NUMB

Text copyright © 2014 Valerie O'Brien

All Rights Reserved

This book is dedicated to you.

IRIS

On the kitchen counter she noticed a silver box. Her name and "Happy Birthday" were written on a tiny card attached to it. He left it there for her to find. She opened the box, revealing an expensive pair of black leather gloves with a soft lining. Iris admired how they fit over her thin, long fingers. As she removed the gloves, yanking the fingertips loose, tears rimmed the corner of her eyes. She blinked repeatedly to keep mascara from streaming along her cheeks. The thought of being in his arms made her sad. She wanted to be happy with Steve like she'd been when things were good between them. True love is a rare gem. Now it hurt to love him. She picked up her cell phone to send him a "Thank you" text and then remembered that it would be hours before he bothered to respond to it. They hadn't talked to each other since the argument. Now it seemed that they always argued over little things. Steve was indifferent with Iris. He cared more about numbers and his friends than her. She was second to everything that happened in his life and he seemed to like it this way.

She grabbed a black wool coat from the closet in the hallway and left the apartment for work. Outside she squinted and lowered her gaze. Mounds of leaves lined the sidewalk and covered the ground. A beautiful array of mandarin, crimson, and chocolate colored, crispy leaves indicative of a season's change. The air outside was cold. Some leaves lifted in the wind as she walked toward her car to open the door. It took a while for the car to warm up inside. Vapors rose as she blew air into her palms and then put on stretch gloves. A few miles into the drive, she took a sip of

3

black coffee. The steam from it warmed the tip
of her nose. Pop music on the radio distracted
thoughts of Steve. She was bitter with him. He
could've given the gift to her. He chose not
to. Closer to work she hurried to finish the
coffee. She veered a little into the left lane
just missing a pothole. Droplets of coffee
landed on the seatbelt and her coat. She wiped
them with a tissue taken from inside the
armrest. High winds whistled against the
windows, making it difficult to keep the car
steady.

In the parking lot she saw an open space
close to the entrance and this made her smile.
She wouldn't have to walk far in heels. She
pulled into the parking space, turned off the
ignition, and sat in silence thinking of how
she would conceal her emotions once she passed
beyond the steel door. None of her employees
knew that it was her birthday or the sadness
it brought her for having one. Her long hair,
brown and curly, lifted in cold winds as she
walked toward the entrance. Black patent
leather heels clanked on the pavement. One
strap to a burgundy leather tote bag slid off
her right shoulder. She frowned and pushed the
strap up and decked herself in the chin with
the other purse dangling from her left arm. As
soon as she reached the front door to the
building, the strap fell down again. She
entered with a few other employees. Another
person held the door open for them. Iris was
startled by a woman standing in the lobby
area. She wore a tight fitting business suit
with pleaser shoes. They were open-toe,
strappy, black leather with clear six-inch
stiletto heels. The multi-colored scarf that
hung loosely around her neck didn't mask her
ample cleavage.

4

She was curious about the woman, but not enough to inquire who she was or what she was doing in the building. Maybe she was meeting someone or she worked there in one of the businesses on a different floor. She thought of saying something about her scarf in hopes of engaging in conversation with the mystery woman. She feared she might learn something that she didn't want to know. It was a phobia that prevented her from closeness with anyone other than Steve. The woman had a pretty face, a clear dark complexion, and she wore a long, dark blonde wig. Their eyes met, she forced a smile, and that was it. Iris turned her attention to the door that led to the stairwell. She decided to walk to the fifth floor to avoid a ride on a crowded elevator. She needed more time alone before she greeted workers in the bakery. She walked toward the door that led to the stairwell, took a deep breath, and whispered *I am safe*. She imagined herself standing on a sandy beach, listening to ocean waves crash against rocks near the shore. Cool water splashed against her feet and ankles. Sun beams warm her light brown skin. The vision calmed her. It was a method she learned from her doctor. Her heels clanked against metal steps that seemed endless. Winded now, she wished for the courage to ride an elevator again. But she couldn't do it.

The last time Iris rode one she was with several other people. All strangers in a metal box strung by cables, drifting from floor to floor. Her anxiety rose as it lifted and abruptly stopped at each floor. Her ears felt clogged and she had tunnel vision. She feared the elevator walls would collapse on them. Terrified that the others knew her secret from the sweat stain expanding across the back of

her green silk blouse, she suddenly felt
shortness of breath. This always led to a
panic attack. After that day, she vowed to
avoid elevators. She was almost to the top of
the last flight of stairs leading to a white
steel door on the fifth floor. When she
finally placed both feet on the landing at the
top of the stairs, she inhaled long and deep
and then quickly exhaled. Time to give a good
face.

THE BAKERY

"Morning." Everyone working at the back station looked up and greeted her as she entered the bakery. Kevin watched Iris as she walked toward the office and then he smiled at her. She was a slender, radiant, young beauty in her early twenties with freckles across the bridge of her nose. She loved the scent of cake baking in huge stainless steel ovens. The sweet aroma of pound cake and buttercream frosting filled the space. She placed her purse and tote bag on a cherry wood desk in her office. It was organized and spacious. There was a large window with an impeccable view of downtown Chicago. Against one wall was a pleated, burgundy leather sofa with legs trimmed in bronze. She found it at an antique store for a bargain price. The half bathroom was decorated in contemporary style. It was spotless, all white with a tall elongated toilet and a frosted glass sink on top of the vanity. She checked her makeup in the mirror and then changed her shoes. Old running shoes were a comfortable fit and the best option for long hours at the bakery.

She looked out the window and thought of Joan. It was still a shock to her that Joan, the former owner of the bakery and one of her closest friends, died in a car accident and left the business to her. Joan never told Iris that she was in her will, but somehow she knew that she would be happy to take over as the owner and run the place as well as she did. Everyone at the bakery liked her. They were pleased that she was the new boss. She looked around her office to check that everything was in place. She took the white apron off the hook near the door and walked back onto the bakery floor. Music from a local radio station was playing. It was for bakers, not customers. The sound kept them in a cheery mood and moving at a quick pace. Two people were working on mail order cakes for an upcoming wedding and two others were preparing cakes for the storefront. They sold plenty of cakes each day. The most popular one was a triple layer German chocolate cake. Customers loved the coconut pecan icing. It was creamy, sweet, and delicious.

Joan gave Iris the recipe, which was handed down to her from her great aunt. The great aunt was a master baker. Today she couldn't bake with the others. Normally when she felt low, baking made her feel better, but her mind was on Steve. The relationship was in ruin. They were strangers under the same roof. There was nothing he could say or do to remove the pain she felt inside. She didn't want to live with him anymore. The thought of telling him this and then actually leaving him was difficult to do. In one hour the bakery would open and customers would file in for their cakes. Business was profitable. Annually she made a six figure salary. Her employees were well compensated for their work. She ensured that they had an excellent plan for health benefits and retirement. Employees could take the retirement package with them if they ever decided baking was no longer their passion. Joan had always taken care of her employees. She wanted to be that kind of boss too. She believed that bakers had to love flour on clothes and embedded in the crevices of shoes; the smell of cake baking for over eight hours a day; the endless varieties of decorations and icings for every occasion. The pure art of making cakes that people loved and took photos of and remembered for years to come.

A baker's life consumed her. She loved every aspect of it. It was the one thing in her life that was constant and brought happiness. Cake was the only baked item sold in the bakery every day of the week. Sometimes a person from another state would ask, "Why do you only sell cakes and not muffins or pastries too?" Iris would smile and say, "We are The Cake Factory." This was all she had to say to get her point across. Sometimes customers suggested they sell a variety of baked goods and coffee. To that Iris would say, "You can get coffee anywhere in the city. Our cakes are specially made." No one could argue against that fact. For forty years The Cake Factory sold only cakes. They built a good reputation by offering the best cakes in Chicago. When Joan inherited the business, she felt it was best to continue with her family's tradition of baking and selling specialty cakes. Iris updated the look of the bakery and had new workstations installed in the baking area, but she had no interest in changing what they offered.

This morning one of the cakes fell minutes before she arrived to work and instead of remaking the cake alone, she advised two bakers to redo it so that it would be perfect. They were surprised by her reaction. They knew that Iris liked to be in control of any mishaps with cake at the bakery. When something like this occurred, she always fixed the problem. *If he cared about me he would've handed me the gift*. She wondered if he had anything else planned for her birthday. Why hadn't he called to acknowledge that she was a year older? She put both hands in the front pockets of her apron and said, "I'll be in my office if you need me." The first customer who

9

entered the bakery was a tall and stout, middle-aged man. He was there to pick up a tuxedo cake. It was a gift to his wife in celebration of their tenth wedding anniversary.

One of the bakers brought the box upfront and as soon as Joe examined the cake he gasped and said, "There's a mistake." For a moment the two bakers looked confused. One went to retrieve the original order form and the other asked, "What's wrong with the cake?" He pointed to the name on the cake and said, "It's right here." They spent several hours decorating the cake and it was beautifully frosted with whipped vanilla cream and chocolate fudge cascading over the edge. The decoration took time away from preparation of other cake orders for upcoming events happening around the city. A misspelling on a recipient's name was a huge deal. The kind that infuriated Iris more than anything else that could go wrong with a cake. The baker standing near the cash register apologized for the mistake and secretly wished for the other team member to hurry back with the order form. A few other customers walked into the bakery while they were helping Joe. One talked on her cell phone and another thumbed through the cake book. Ray came back with the invoice. Joe looked at it and said, "The order is correct, but as you can see there's an "n" missing from my wife's name. This has to be fixed today. The anniversary party starts in two hours." His face was slightly red and his brow was wrinkled as he leaned into the front counter. Joe shifted his weight and bent his right leg. The left leg was stiff. His fists were clenched and pressed against the counter.

He stared at the two bakers as if to say, *you are going to fix this so that I can walk out of here with what I've already pre-paid for*. Both darted eyes between the order form and cake, then felt a lump form in their throats. Workers at the bakery hadn't made a flub like this one in a long time. When this happened before, it was just as bad. The message on the cake was correct, but the frosting was wrong. They had to make another cake and they delivered it late. Iris lost money on that sale. The bakers feared she might yell at them for sure as soon as she learned of their mistake. Ray, still holding the form, smiled at Joe and assured him that he would take care of the matter. Joe sighed and asked, "How long will it take you to fix the cake?" Ray really didn't know what to say to Joe, but he had to put this customer's mind at ease. Joe was a regular and he frequently recommended the bakery to his clients, which brought them a lot of business. Two customers who had been waiting were becoming impatient and they wanted the matter with Joe, who was holding up the line, resolved.

Stacey decided to help the next customer in line so that she wouldn't have to wait any longer. She was a teenage girl picking up an order of strawberry shortcakes for a sweet sixteen birthday party. Two weeks in advance she requested sixteen of them, one for each guest at her party. The order was filled quickly and without any problems. When she opened the door to leave, the bells on it chimed. Her auburn ponytail swung back and forth as she motioned out of view. Stacey noticed Ray struggling to keep Joe's temper from flaring and knew that she had to get Iris. Her palms were sweaty as she thought of telling her boss about the problem with the man's cake. If anyone could clear things up, Iris was the one to do it. She tapped on the office door and entered once she heard Iris say, "Come in." Without hesitation Stacey told her the news. Iris crossed one arm across her chest and let her elbow on the other arm rest on it. She covered one eye with her hand after hearing Stacey recount the incident. Clearly, she was perturbed by their mistake, but she knew how to fix it. Iris needed the distraction. She greeted Joe with a warm welcome and asked him to join them on the bakery floor.

Customers were rarely invited to watch bakers work. But this was an exception that had to happen. She believed that if Joe saw how hard they worked in the bakery this would soften his mood as he waited for them to fix his anniversary cake. The cake was cold and when handled carefully, the icing could be removed. Iris took out a metal pick from her apron and gently lifted off each letter. The bakers were amazed at how easily the letters came off. Joe was astonished by her skill. When she lifted the "i", a piece of cake came off with it. Stacey's eyes widened and her heart raced as she wondered what her boss would do next. Everyone else kept working and occasionally they looked up to watch Iris transform the cake. At this point, none of the bakers would dare attempt to fix the icing.

One baker tried this lifting method and had icing and cake lifting simultaneously, which ruined it beyond repair so they had to remake the entire cake. "Bring me the bin with chocolate cake scraps," Iris said in a low voice. Joe watched and waited patiently for her to finish the cake. He crossed his left leg over the other one and rested clasped fingers near a brown tweed hat on his lap. The hat matched his brown leather dress shoes. Joe's face was no longer red. Ray returned to the work station with a small bin of cake scraps. She broke off tiny pieces of chocolate cake to fill the hole on top of the cake. It was artfully done. Each piece of cake was meticulously placed. The others were quiet now and weren't as busy as they were pretending to be when the boss began fixing the cake.

They were staring at her, hopeful about the process. "Bring me the chocolate ganache," she said. She sculpted the tiny section on the top of the cake so perfectly it looked as if there was never anything wrong with the cake at all. Iris replaced the letters with new ones and correctly spelled Jennifer. "Joe, your cake is ready." He looked at the tuxedo cake and smiled. "You'll have to place it in the refrigerator for an hour so that the icing really sets in this spot," she said while pointing at it. "Thank you, my wife will love it." Ray and Stacey let out a sigh of relief. Calmness was restored in everyone as Joe left the baking area. Meanwhile the store front was busy with orders to be filled and for now the drama was over. Iris walked back to the office to check emails and be alone for a while.

STEVE

He left her birthday gift on the kitchen counter so that he wouldn't have to interact with her. While she slept, he watched her. She looked beautiful. Serene. Iris was a bitch. They were strangers to each other. Some mornings Steve tried to make small talk with her, but she never seemed to be in the mood to listen to his concerns or add to the conversation. He felt dead inside. All she wanted to do was end their relationship. A week before her birthday they argued about her unwillingness to give counseling a try. "Why should I allow a doctor to psychoanalyze my feelings?" she said. He banged his fist against the kitchen cabinet, rattling white ceramic dishes stacked inside. Iris continued to sip her coffee and mindlessly flip through a newspaper. "I don't want to do this with you anymore," she said then walked into the bedroom to finish her makeup and put on her heels.

Until now Steve never imagined a life without her. He took off his suit and flung it across the carpeted floor in the living room. If she was there instead of on her way to the bakery she would have picked up his clothes and placed them in the hamper. Their apartment was always clean and tidy. She made certain that it stayed in this condition. *Everything has its place* was a mantra for Iris. He was annoyed by it and would shift things around in the apartment, small things like placing his toothbrush on the right side instead of the left side of the vanity in the bathroom. Or he'd move a framed photo on the mantle in the living room a few inches out of its original position. He inhaled her scent as he lied alone in bed. Angry and confused, he withheld tears. She had no right to give up on him. He was certain she noticed things like this and probably put everything he moved back in its proper place according to her standards, but it didn't matter. Steve felt in control and like the victor when he moved things around. He had given her his all and if that wasn't good enough then perhaps this truly was the end for them.

On his day off, he drove to the lakefront. He always felt better after a long run. He wanted to run away from emotional pain. The morning air was cool. He pulled a navy blue hood over his head and then realized he left his iPod. It didn't matter; he needed the run more than music. There weren't many others on the path. He liked that. Cyclists were the ones to watch out for. They ride so fast and weave in and out to avoid walkers and runners, but someone always gets clipped and this leads to a domino effect of people stumbling over one another.

It happened to him last month. A man on a marathon bike, wearing a bright yellow and green training outfit raced toward two women walking on the path. Steve heard the biker shout at them to move out of the way. He had to go between them to avoid hitting someone. The women didn't hear him until the last minute. It was too late, although they spread apart to let him go through. By this time, the cyclist decided to veer left and he clipped one of the women, down she went, and he followed her. His bike wheel landed on Steve's left side. It hit his shoulder and scraped his leg. Steve got up to help the woman on the ground. Her walking partner did the same. She was fine, only startled by the accident. The biker apologized to them.

Steve walked along the path for a few minutes to warm-up his muscles. He was naturally lean and in excellent physical condition for a man in his mid-forties. His mid-section was tight and his quads were ripped. He believed he looked great in a pair of khaki walking shorts. Iris didn't appreciate his physique. As he trotted, he searched his memory for the last time he clasped hands with her, walked in sync along the lakefront. The first year of their relationship they often did this. Iris wouldn't hesitate to leave the bakery to go for a stroll with Steve on his lunch break. He missed the times she seemed so in love with him she couldn't keep her hands off him. The relationship was solid. On long walks they talked about their day and plans for their future together.

Now, Iris would never do anything like this with him. He ran a little faster and the wind felt cool against his skin. The woman running toward Steve was shapely and quite attractive. She nodded at Steve as she ran past him. She had on a pink top, light grey spandex pants, and white running shoes. She was wearing a khaki cap with the words "Go Hard" on it. She smiled at him as she ran past. He felt like she was flirting and he really liked this. It felt wonderful to be acknowledged for a change. It gave him confidence. His woman hadn't flirted with him in over a year. The intimacy was gone. A peck on the lips in the morning before they both left for work was obsolete. Hugs were out of the question. Tears streamed on his face. Light rain fell. Steve ran even faster and perspired heavily. He always ran five miles. On this day, he ran ten. He was tired and winded as he slowly walked back to his car. He checked his phone and there were no messages from Iris.

THE OFFICE

Iris plopped on the sofa in the office. She rubbed her forehead and closed her eyes. She wasn't physically tired. She was mentally exhausted from life with Steve. The bakery was doing well and financially she was more than comfortable. Unhappiness weighted her thoughts. Her cell phone vibrated in her apron pocket. There was a message from him. The text said, "Why are you doing this to us?" She turned off the cell phone and let it drop to the floor. She could care less about his feelings. Every other day he wanted an explanation for the reasons why she wanted out of their relationship. She didn't feel like going over it anymore with him. She felt he was mature enough to deal with his own emotions over the fact that her love was lost and there was nothing either one of them could do about it. She wanted to cry. The tears wouldn't fall. She spent many nights lying next to him wide awake in bed mulling over this matter. She cried alone countless times in other rooms of their apartment. Her tear ducts were closed for business.

When she had days off from the bakery, she spent half of the day crying alone in their bedroom. She thought about the five years they had lived together and wondered how they got to this place. Love was an outsider. When compassion for Steve welled up inside her, Iris reminded herself that everything was his entire fault. Buried deep within her soul was the love she denied. It was a way for her to avoid the truth. The truth was that the failure of their relationship wasn't completely his fault. She was at fault too for allowing herself to give up. When she wanted to discuss or work through things that had

17

gone wrong in their relationship, he often
brushed her off. It hurt that Steve repeatedly
did this to her. To make up for it he once
asked her to go with him to seek guidance from
a pastor. One of his friends recommended it.
An odd request from someone who wasn't
religious. They went to weddings held at
various churches. But they never attended
church for any other reason. When he expressed
that he hoped doing this would help save their
relationship, she agreed to it, although she
went with a guarded heart and mind.

CHURCH

Three years ago they arrived at Greater Union Baptist Church on a sunny Wednesday morning. Steve wore a tan business suit and Iris had on a fitted vintage black dress. She wore pearls with dangling pearl and diamond encrusted earrings to match. Lace stockings peeked through open-toe black patent leather heels. A pearl bracelet with a gold clasp was on her left wrist. On the other wrist she had a silver, diamond encrusted watch. The jewelry was an anniversary gift from Steve. The dress clung to her curves. The car was filled with a sweet floral fragrance. It was a nice day. They didn't say one word to each other in the car ride on the way to the church. This bothered Steve and he couldn't keep silent about it. "Are you going to a funeral?" he said. *Here we go.* "The way our relationship feels right now is like we may as well be dead to each other," she said without looking at him. Her words were a blade's edge, cutting deep into his core. Silence was best.

When they arrived, He sent a text and checked his emails before they met Pastor John. He thought of all the nicer things she could've said to him in the car, like how handsome he looked in his designer suit or how close he got with his shave. Steve's brown skin almost glowed, but she didn't notice. He wished she hadn't said anything at all. But as soon as they were ready to enter the church, she had to say something mean. He was angry and irritated with her for the remark. Iris smirked because she knew she had hurt his feelings. He was also guilty of saying mean things to her. They often did things like this to each other to rile each other up. One day he told her she was gaining weight and that she might want to consider eating less carbs for breakfast. She loved bagels. All types of bagels. Her favorite was cinnamon raisin. She loved bread period. For breakfast, she routinely had a whole bagel spread with cream cheese or butter. Steve's comment about her weight made her rethink eating an entire bagel. From that moment on she only ate half a bagel twice a week.

In the beginning of their relationship, she gave up many things just to please him. She wasn't bothered by this at all. She loved him enough to do whatever it would take to keep him happy. The pastor was seated in his office. When he was ready to receive them, the secretary, a short lady with wiry grey hair and a kind face, led them into his office. Pastor John, an older man with dark skin and speckled grey hair, was a soft-spoken, gentle man. He was a widower. Pastor John rose from his seat and extended his hand to them both one at a time. Iris and Steve were standing near the chairs in front of the Pastor's desk. "I'm so glad you've come to see me," he said and then smiled. They all sat down. The Pastor had his bible open and read aloud a few scriptures. They listened and Steve's heart softened. She felt uneasy. She wondered if the Pastor would give a sermon. He laid his hand on top of hers. His hands were strong and veiny. Surprised by his action, she flinched. She liked the warmth of his palm.

As the Pastor spoke to them about love and relationships Iris drifted into a daydream. She imagined the Pastor's life with his wife. Shirley was a pretty woman. She was intelligent and an excellent cook. She made the best roasted potatoes and peppers she'd ever eaten. When she was alive, Shirley invited them to a banquet honoring the Pastor for his work in the community. Pastor John helped the city raise enough funds to open a park. Neighborhood kids who lived on the West Side of the city were grateful for the park. It made the community seem normal like in more affluent areas. It gave them some place to go where they could swing, ride bikes, run around, or even just lay out in the grass and watch clouds shape shift. The Pastor was a good man. Iris thought he probably made his wife a happy woman. Shirley always seemed to be happy and content. It was as if she never had any stress in her life.

She wondered how Shirley died. She couldn't ask the Pastor about his wife's death, although she desperately wanted to know the cause. Iris and Steve weren't regular churchgoers. She could count the number of times they had gone to church on one hand. When they attended church, she never wore black. This was a happier time for them. A time when she wanted nothing more than to be with him for an eternity. She wanted to have children and raise them together with him. Pastor John had one son, Kendall who was a brain surgeon. Iris was friends with Kendall's girlfriend, Kim. They often worked out together. Kim was tall with short brown hair cut into a bob style. Her arms were skinny and muscular. She looked like a fitness model. Kim always talked about healthy eating and exercise, but she suffered from bulimia. While they were having lunch, Kim told Iris about her food binges. She loved fast food, especially cheeseburgers and fries. One night at Mel's drive thru Kim ordered enough food to feed a family of four. She ate everything in a hurry and then in less than an hour later she forced herself to vomit. Iris made a promise that she wouldn't tell anyone about Kim's battle with bulimia.

If Kendall discovered Kim's secret, she feared he might change his mind about the marriage proposal and then cancel the wedding. Iris felt Kim's impression of Kendall was a bit shallow. She didn't think Pastor John, being the gentle man that he was, would have a son who could be insensitive to his future wife. What did she really know about the Pastor? Or how he had raised his son? She knew very little about her own boyfriend she had been with for five years. Pastor John's voice slowly rose above the one in her head and she zoned in from daydreaming. "At this moment, what do you think is the biggest problem in your relationship?" he asked. "There's no intimacy." She couldn't believe the words that flew out of her mouth. It needed to be said, but she had no idea that she had the courage to share her sentiment with the Pastor. Steve removed his hand off hers and tensed up his body in the seat. "We have tension because she's moody and uptight." They were experts at the blame game. His accusation made her uncomfortable.

In this instance, she chose to focus on the facts, although she could've easily retorted with all the things Steve did and didn't do to serve as an explanation for her moodiness. She couldn't imagine the Pastor knowing anything about sex. He was a man of the cloth and much older than them. He couldn't possibly be getting any action. "This has nothing to do with sex. We do it once or twice a week," he said. Iris crossed her legs and said, "He's a bunny rabbit on top while I lie there motionless." He wasn't affectionate with her. Sex was routine. She told the Pastor how he used to rub her shoulders, listen to her talk about the troubles at the bakery, and gently kiss her neck while holding her in his arms. She expressed how much she missed the times when she came home from a long day at the bakery and he would massage her feet, warm her dinner, and then they would eat together. "I still do this, he said." When he interrupted her, she glared at him for a moment, wanted to call him a liar.

She continued sharing her thoughts with Pastor John. She was fearless as she spoke freely about her innermost feelings. She stripped Steve of his power. The fact that he believed he was still as affectionate toward her as he was at the start of their relationship proved that his sense of reality was warped. The Pastor saw the tension between them. The wedge between them spanned wider than the sea. For this initial visit, he thought it was best to let them air out their concerns so that he could gain a clearer understanding of the matter in order to help them restore the love they'd forgotten how to nurture. He asked them to join hands with him as he prayed for them. Afterwards he suggested they come back regularly to see him for couples counseling. He also recommended they read a few Bible scriptures together each night before retiring to bed. They didn't have a Bible. As they left the church, she knew she had chosen the right color dress for the occasion. They never returned to see Pastor John.

UNRAVEL

Steve was furious. He wanted to shake some sense into her. He also wanted to let her have it, really tell her off. The bunny rabbit comment echoed in his mind. He couldn't believe she said that. What else was he supposed to do? Force her to move in the act? If he said anything to her as they walked briskly back to the car, she was prepared with an arsenal of curse words especially for him. With tight lips he glared at her for a brief moment then started the car. She looked straight ahead, ignoring his heavy sighs, all negative energy from him. "Well, I suppose that went swell for you," he said. Iris remained silent. She wasn't going to be goaded into an argument with him. "What is it that you want from me? I'm a good man who does everything for you and yet you are distant toward me, treating me like a stranger. Somewhere things went wrong between us and I feel like I'm the only one trying to get us back on track."

While he spoke, she listened and still remained silent. The anger mixed with pain in his voice was authentic. It didn't eliminate the pain she felt deep within her soul. For a long time her heart ached for him. She felt it was too late for them three years ago when they went to see the Pastor as it was now five years later. Steve pulled the car over to the nearest curb, slammed on the brakes, and turned on the emergency lights. They were near the bakery. She could get out the car and run there. Stay overnight until he calmed down. She knew there was no way to avoid a discussion with him. He was persistent regarding matters he wished to resolve. She used to love this quality about him. At the moment his pushing only made her feel more resentment toward him. Iris took a deep breath and decided to let out a rant. "I don't know that I want anything at all from you. I'm sick and tired of being sick and tired in life with you!" She turned her body slightly and peered directly into his eyes. "For years, it's been all about you and not us. You spend so much time at the office and then afterwards you hang out most nights of the week with your friends. We haven't gone running together or said more than a few words to each other. Years ago the counseling thing was a mistake and I should've never agreed to it. *Breathe.* What good did it do? Everything has to be done on your terms," she said and then turned to face the windshield, watching traffic and people go by.

He listened to her complaints and in many ways he recognized where he had been wrong. She was right. He was glad that she at least shared this with him. For a change she showed some real emotion as if she still cared for him and she hadn't done that in a long time. "I promise to do better. To be there for you more," he said. He let out a long sigh, put the car in drive, and headed for home on the North Side of Chicago. She kept her attention on the lake front. Watching the waves calmed her mood. She was emotional and all she wanted to do was take a hot bath at home and fall asleep. Steve asked to run her bath water. She knew he was trying to make up with her, to be close to her again.

A memory surfaced of them in the bathtub. They used to take baths together. *Nothing better than laughter and bubbles with your lover.* He cradled her in his arms until they were wrinkled and the water turned cold. They did everything together. Friends believed they were inseparable. They were wrong. No one knew their relationship was in trouble. Iris didn't tell Carol, her closest friend, about her troubles with him. Each time they talked on the phone she avoided Carol's questions about her personal life.

They entered the apartment in silence. Steve flushed the toilet and leaned over the tub. "I can run my own water. Give me some space," she said. He left her alone to undress in the bathroom. She used to undress in front of him without care of him staring at her. He loved to look at her smooth, brown body. Her curves, the way her hair moved across her back as she removed her push up bra. He stood in the bathroom doorway for a few minutes. She liked being watched and wanted to give into the trace of love that loomed over them. Tears formed in her eyes, but she blinked them back. She leaned over the tub and turned the water on. When the water was the right temperature, she put the stopper in.

Steve closed the door. Iris pressed three squirts of her favorite bath soap in the tub. The bubbles quickly rose. She inhaled the scent of lavender and felt steam against her skin. She sat on the edge of the tub and let the water rise just below the spout. Shiny silver knobs squeaked as she turned the water off. She immersed her left foot in bubbly water. It was hot. She resisted taking it out. Slowly she put her right foot in and enjoyed the sting of hot water against her skin. As she lowered herself in the tub, she felt weightless and warm all over. She closed her eyes and tried to let worry and stress disappear. The Pastor was no help. She couldn't tell her friend Carol. She wasn't sure how to handle it. She soaked in the tub for a few hours that night. When she came out, he was sound asleep. She was relieved to find him like that. It meant she didn't have to talk to or reject affection from him.

When she lifted the cover and lied next to him, he didn't move. The bed was firm, yet soft enough to cradle her body. The smell of his cologne was masculine and nice. Normally, each night he showered and brushed his teeth before bed. She felt bad for taking so long in the bathroom. He once filled her heart with happiness. They used to fill each other's lives with bliss. That lasted for two years. By the third year of their live-in arrangement, darkness altered the way they interacted with each other. Even the minor things he did bothered her. She liked order and he was well aware of how obsessively neat she was and how everything had to be in its proper place. If he moved a book from the coffee table she noticed and complained until he put it back. She knew if his socks were out of place. Each pair was rolled and tucked neatly in the top dresser drawer and arranged by color, length, and texture. His side of the closet was meticulously organized by color and style. Outer wear was hung on matching black coat hangers in the closet near the front door.

Their apartment was huge. Two thousand square feet of space that was sparsely decorated with modern furniture. On this issue they agreed. When they looked at the place, they fell in love with dark hardwood floors and the terrace with a view of Lake Michigan. The modern kitchen had stainless steel appliances and large glass tiles for the back splash. The bathroom had double sinks and a whirlpool tub on one side. There was free standing shower with natural stone tile encased in glass. Steve was enthusiastic about the entire design of the place. He even mentioned that the apartment was large enough for them to start a family one day. Iris wasn't nervous by his remark back then. She welcomed the experience. Now on the verge of a break up she couldn't entertain the thought of having children. She drifted into a deep sleep.

THERAPY

At the bakery someone knocked on the office door. Iris shifted her body on the sofa, tried to ignore the sound, and fall asleep again. Kevin called her phone. He was one of her funniest employees. "Hey, we're trying to run a business here so there will be no sleeping on the job. Unless I can nap too." She smiled and walked toward the door to unlock it. He told her that he wanted to deliver a wedding cake early. The flow of customers in the store had slowed some and he had an extra hour before the cake was scheduled for delivery. On the way back he also wanted to grab lunch for everyone at Sandwich Hut, which is the real reason he woke her. He wanted her permission. He liked looking at his boss. She granted his request and added her sandwich to the order list. Sandwich Hut had the best turkey sandwiches in the downtown area. The roasted turkey was juicy and tender. She liked hers on a whole grain wheat bun with Swiss cheese, mustard, mayonnaise, lettuce, tomato, and red onion. It had to be made exactly in this way otherwise she wouldn't eat it.

She told him to call the wedding cake recipients to let them know that the cake would be delivered early. Iris would later learn how pleased the customers were to have received it in advance. They sent the staff a bottle of Armand de Brignac with a thank you card. The wedding couple had wealthy parents on both sides of the family. The only reason she agreed to let him deliver the cake to them early was because she knew they had a large restaurant style refrigerator at the banquet hall where they were having the wedding ceremony and reception. A wedding cake should not sit for an hour at room temperature. The icing would soften too much and the topper would shift and probably fall off. Iris couldn't return to sleep so she decided to organize old customer order slips. She kept her files in two cherry wood file cabinets. Customer slips were kept for one year. After a year they were shredded at the local office supply store. Customer orders were documented in a spread sheet that showed the customer's information, payment, and date received. The paper copy was a backup source in case technology ever failed. She also made certain to back up all computer files daily on a separate hard drive.

Iris recalled one time her former boss lost almost all the customer files when a power outage shut down everything in the bakery. Joan didn't have an external hard drive with those files on it. There was information about customer orders from people who had been loyal patrons since the bakery opened its doors for business. Joan was sick over the loss. She took the computer to a technician and he was able to retrieve some of the lost information, but not all of it. After that incident she learned how to backup all customer files so it would never happen again. Joan lost quite a bit of sleep over the matter, although she found several hundred customer numbers and orders in a book she kept. When the owner died, Iris placed the book in her coffin. She would have liked knowing they did this for her. Iris hated clutter which is why she got rid of old files after one year. Leaning on the cabinet, she took a moment to admire her office space. It had plenty of room to move around in. There was a tap on the door. She knew it wasn't

Kevin. He hadn't been gone long enough;
besides, he had to drop off the wedding cake
first.

It was Tina, her chatty baker, who wanted
to talk. She was a sweet young woman in her
early twenties. She had worked at the bakery
for a few years. She was going to culinary
arts school to be a pastry chef. Tina truly
loved to bake. She could measure flour while
blindfolded. She was gifted at freehand
writing on cakes. Iris knew that Tina wanted
to talk about her fiancé. Iris thought she was
too young to get married, but she knew there
was no way to convince her of this, especially
once her fiancé put a 5-carat diamond on her
tiny ring finger. She opened the door and
smiled at her. Tina was pretty. She wore light
blue skinny jeans and a yellow top with the
number twenty-one on the front of it. Tina
smiled and looked at the sofa in the office.
Iris motioned for her to come in.
"How are you feeling today?"
"I'm fine and how are you?"
"The same as always, a bit tired, but I just
ignore the feeling."
"Have a seat."

Tina sat on the sofa and Iris sat in the
chair near the desk. She wanted to twirl in
it, but resisted as this would appear rude and
show that she wasn't interested in what Tina
had to share. She let out a long sigh and told
Iris her parents didn't believe that her
fiancé was the right man for her. She didn't
understand why they felt this way about him.
"From the start they seemed to like him," she
said. He was smart and wealthy. Not that her
parents were gold diggers, but they wanted
their daughter to marry someone who was
financially stable enough to take care of her.

"We had dinner at a Hibachi restaurant and things were going smoothly until he mentioned the prenuptial agreement. I was caught off guard. This was something that he and I had only discussed once in our relationship." They had been together for three years and engaged for the past year. "Uh, oh. How'd that go?"

"I felt he was out of line, blurting this news at dinner with my parents. I hadn't thought of the prenup since he mentioned it in casual conversation two years ago," she said. "What was his motive for telling your parents?" Tina shook her head as if to say no and then leaned forward on the sofa, placing one hand over her forehead. "I don't really know. There was so much tension at the dinner table once the nuptial agreement was out in the open. We all sat quiet for a while, waiting for the food to arrive. I tried to lighten the mood by asking my parents how they planned to spend the rest of their evening. It was a stretch for anything I could think of to divert their attention from being upset with me, which was quite obvious from concerned looks on their faces. And my fiancé stayed on the phone, taking call after unimportant call. "That's rude."

"My mother nearly choked on her glass of white wine when she heard the news. She didn't understand his rationale for wanting me to sign a prenuptial. My dad felt the same way, but his irritation with my fiancé was worse than mine. I'm not some charity case. My dad worked hard all his life to make money. He was insulted that my fiancé overlooked the fact that my father provided for his family without anyone's help. I was disappointed that he shared this with them without telling me first prior to dinner."

"Have you spoken to him about it?" Tina kept her gaze on the floor and shook her head for no.

"What made him do this?" Tina sighed and said, "I really don't know." She complained about her trouble for a little while longer, but Iris knew that she wasn't going to let the nuptial agreement ruin her chances of having a fancy wedding. She hadn't picked out a wedding dress. They needed to set a date for it. When they tried to agree on one, her fiancé always made excuses about the location, food, or how many guests could attend the wedding.

Iris thought the fiancé was a jerk. The entire time she listened while Tina talked she thought of options for advice to give her. She decided it was best to avoid asking questions to remain neutral about the matter. She wasn't the type to get involved in her employees' personal lives. Her life with Steve wasn't great anymore. She was no guru at relationships. Iris wanted to ask Tina, "What kind of guy would tell his future in-laws that he wants their daughter to sign a prenuptial before discussing it with her?" She thought Tina should've ended the relationship that night. In silence she sat behind her desk and stared at Tina who was still looking at the floor. Tina began crying. Iris didn't notice it until she cried louder, heaving as she scooted backward on the sofa then, put her head to her knees, covering it with both arms.

She was hesitant to go to her side. Should she go over and hug her? Wipe her tears? Or should she give her the space to let it all out? Maybe a good cry would make her feel better. She didn't want to be insensitive to her feelings. She knew what Tina was going through. Iris walked over to the sofa and sat next to her. She decided silence was best and cradled her in her arms, letting her cry until her emotions were under control. The top of her blouse and apron strap were soaked with salty tears. Her phone rang inside the apron pocket. Iris knew who it was before she lifted and silenced it. Steve always called several times a day. Sometimes he wanted to ask her out to lunch or dinner. Other times he wanted to vent about his job. He was a good accountant. Balancing budgets was a no-brainer for him. She had no interest in listening to him anymore. Tina apologized for being needy and crying on her boss's designer blouse. "I'm just so torn about us now." She sniffled. "I feel that I shouldn't have to sign a stupid agreement. My love should be enough to withstand some paper saying that I won't take half of his assets if we get divorced. Why doesn't he see that this is a mistake and that we should focus on why we decided to get married in the first place? I want to marry for love and not money." Tina was trying to convince herself and her boss, who was silent, sitting next to her and listening to her rant.

In her heart, Tina knew that her fiancé cared most about his large sum of inheritance money. She wiped her nose with the tissue Iris gave her when she began the crying spell. Tina hears her cell phone ringing. It's her fiancé. She quickly answers it before the ringing ends. Iris remains quiet until she's finished her conversation. "How are you doing at the bakery? Would you like to grab lunch?" he said. "Everything is fine here. I'm in the office talking to my boss." He was suspicious of her tone. "Are you getting sick? It sounds like you're coming down with a cold or worse the flu." She paced the office while talking

34

to him. Iris watched her walk across the carpet, a paisley print rug, and then back onto the carpet. "Well, I have to get back to the bakery floor." She didn't, but he let her get off the phone. At that moment Iris noticed tiny scars on the inside of Tina's arm. She stared at them.

Normally, she was careful around others she worked with and kept her arms close to her body while she worked to hide the scars. Tina looked as if she had seen a ghost. She felt uncomfortable now that her secret was exposed. Iris walked toward her to get a closer look. The cuts were thin incisions going in various directions like abstract art on the inside of her forearm. When she noticed her boss looking at her arm, she covered it with the other hand. "Why do you do this?"
"I don't know. It makes me feel better. I haven't done it for a long time." As she told Iris this she realized that she was making up excuses to mask the true reason she began cutting herself. She was unhappy about her fiancé trying to force her to sign a prenuptial agreement. She felt that it was a mistake to continue being with him, but she was too much of a coward to end the relationship. Iris' eyes narrowed as she listened to Tina. "So are you saying that cutting yourself helps to take your attention off the things that are troubling you?" She nodded her head in agreement.

Iris felt she should say something to this young girl to help her end the self-mutilation. She didn't know what to say to make her stop. Nothing profound came to her. They stood in silence for a brief moment. Tina's eyes were brimming with tears. Iris knew that hugging her tightly was better than words. She held her for a long time. Tina felt comfort, knowing that her boss truly cared about her feelings. She believed she was crazy and in need of someone to talk to; someone she could trust with her personal information; someone who wouldn't spread her business to others at the bakery, although they were like a family. Others suspected she had been cutting herself. She really didn't try to conceal it. She always wore short-sleeved shirts to work. The cuts weren't deep or wide, but they were quite obvious.

Tina left the office feeling better than she did when she came in. It was one hour until closing time and the bakery had slowed with customers. All cakes for the day had been delivered. The orders for delivery or pickup were ready for the next day. Employees on the bakery floor were putting away boxes and cake scraps in plastic bins. A new worker dropped a huge metal mixing bowl filled with vanilla crème frosting. Several gasps could be heard from others. Someone even smacked their lips over the incident. Iris didn't say anything about the matter. She kept organizing the scrap bins by cake type. Kevin wondered if something was wrong with her.

Today she was too quiet and withdrawn. On most days when she arrived at the bakery, she worked some from the office and later came out to help on the bakery floor or in the store front. Her cell phone vibrated in her apron pocket. It was Steve calling her again. She knew he would call a second time after not receiving an answer from her about dinner. She answered the phone in a pleasant voice. "Hello, how are you?" He paused from shock. He thought who was this woman on the other end of his girlfriend's cell phone? "H—hi, you caught me off guard."

"I know I did. So I was thinking we should have dinner at that Japanese restaurant downtown. I can meet you there in about an hour." He was confused, but he liked her suggestion. He thought for sure she would say no to dinner. He was surprised that he didn't have to beg her to accept his offer. "Sure, it's a great idea." They confirmed the time to meet and said goodbye before the call ended. Kevin couldn't resist mentioning the date she arranged with her boyfriend. "Since you have a hot date tonight maybe you should take a few pieces of cake for dessert." This made her giggle. She liked his humor and wit. She was watching him as he walked over to the refrigerated food area, imagining what it would be like in a relationship with him. He was in his early thirties, over six feet tall and lean. Shirts clung to his abs. She traced his strong arms with her gaze as he walked out back to dump the trash. Locked in her thoughts she didn't notice the bakery floor was being swept by another baker. Kevin was younger than her. He liked to date older women. The sweeper nudged her to move out the way. Iris gathered her belongings from the office and said, "Have a good evening" to her employees and left.

FIX IT

She smelled like lemon cake. It was the last one sold to an older woman who needed it for her book club meeting. While she walked toward her car parked in back of the bakery, she thought of the things she might say to her soon to be ex-boyfriend. She wanted him to know that she cared enough about him to want to end the relationship on a positive note. Maybe they could be friends. He wouldn't go for that. He would try to convince her that this was a rough phase in their relationship and that they should seek couples counseling again before making a final decision. She wanted to cancel the dinner date when she thought of having to face Steve and the reality of a breakup. She received a text from him that said he was going to be a little late due to traffic. She had the same problem. Traffic was bumper to bumper on the way to the restaurant. It was a sign of how long the evening was going to be. What would it be like at home for them after dumping him at dinner?

She tapped her fingers on the steering wheel while listening to a favorite song on a rhythm and blues radio station. She turned the volume up. She sang a few words and bobbed her head to the music. Stress ascended from her shoulders. Stalled traffic was no longer a worry. She decided not to cower from the truth or live with the regret of knowing that she stayed with him because Steve appeared to be a good man. When she veered toward the exit ramp near the restaurant, tiny beads of sweat collected under her armpits. Her entire body warmed. She was trembling. She took slow, deep breaths in hopes of trying to calm her nerves. *How will I greet him?* The parking lot adjacent to the restaurant was filled with luxury vehicles. She circled the block a few times before she finally landed a parking space on the street not far from the restaurant. Her stomach rumbled a bit as she entered through revolving glass doors.

Inside the place was dark and decorated in authentic Japanese style. Soft lighting from round paper lamps hung overhead. The food smelled divine. Steve was at the bar nursing a cocktail, waiting for her arrival. Like always, he was impressively dressed in a suit. He looked handsome. It was a tailored grey one with white pin stripes. In his eyes, Iris saw humility and weariness. The love he felt for her was apparent. He smiled, happy to see her and asked if she wanted to dine in the outside seating area. She agreed to it. When she arrived, he avoided the urge to embrace her after she walked over to him at the bar. Normally, he does this and kisses her on the cheek. He left a tip for the cute bartender who had been flirting with him until she noticed his date. Something about his demeanor made Iris uncomfortable. He didn't seem desperate to cater to her in every way. He allowed her to lead the way through open glass sliding doors. Outside the weather was warm with an occasional cool breeze. They sat down and looked at the menus already on the table.

A waiter came over immediately after they seated themselves. He was weird looking. He had a huge nose and a weak chin. His hair was dyed black, but he was a natural blond. She could tell from the outgrowth that he needed a touch-up in color. His eyes were pale blue and he had on heavy black eyeliner. His fingernails were painted black and on his wrist he wore multiple thin, black rubber bands. He wore a spotless white apron and this

is something Iris expected from the wait staff
at any restaurant. If the apron or shoes were
overly dirty with food, she felt the place was
unclean and the food wasn't safe to consume.
Steve was also particular about food safety
when considering a restaurant. He thought the
guy looked weird too because of his gothic
style, but he didn't give the guy a hard time.
"Hello, my name is Josh. I'll be your server
this evening. What can I start you off with?"
She ordered a glass of white wine. "And for
you, sir, can I refresh your drink?"
"No, I'm fine for now." The waiter jerked his
head back to flip hair covering his eye.
"I'll give you some time to look over the menu
then I'd be delighted to take your order." He
was working on getting a more than decent tip
from them. Steve smiled and nodded in
acknowledgement. As he walked off Iris noticed
the waiter was wearing black skinny jeans that
stopped right above his ankles. For a few
moments they sat in silence, waiting for one
or the other to start the conversation. Steve
took a sip of his drink and said, "So overall
how was your day?"
"It was busy at the bakery. One of the bakers
misspelled a customer's name."
"I know you fixed it perfectly and you've
probably gained a lifelong customer."
"I guess so."
"Did you go out for lunch?"
"One of the bakers grabbed food for us. I had
a sub sandwich and Coke."
They were being polite to each other with
small talk. Iris hated small talk. The reason
they were having dinner would soon surface. He
was overly relaxed. She tapped her foot
underneath the table. She appeared to be fine.
Internally she was hiding true feelings. He

knew she would attempt to end their relationship and he was waiting for her to say it. The waiter returned. His bangs were no longer covering his left eye. He stared at Iris for more than a few minutes. He was feeling her out. The waiter thought she was attractive and if he saw an opening, he had already planned how he would give her his number. She picked up on this and was flattered. He wasn't her type and he was too young for her. What would people say if they saw the two of them hanging out? "Are you ready to order?" She ordered sushi and he had teriyaki chicken. While they waited for dinner cool winds blew against her skin. She realized she still had on the clothes she'd worn to work and wished for a different outfit. He leaned his knee against hers under the table. He extended his hand with hopes that she would accept this gesture. She could feel the warmth in his strong hands and it opened her heart.

With the events of the day whirling in her mind and the pressure to stay with a man she didn't know anymore, she let tears drop. He squeezed her left hand a little tighter. She wiped her eyes with a napkin. Steve didn't say a word. He wanted to pour out his heart to her again, but resisted in fear that it would do little to sway her decision. Early in life one thing he learned about a woman was that when she cries it's best to leave her alone. He never bothered his mother when he saw her cry. He wanted to comfort Iris and let her know that he would try to be understanding of her feelings. He wanted her to know that her feelings were valid; that he would listen even if it meant losing her. On the other hand, he also wanted to smack her across one of those

perfectly blushed high cheekbones and tell her
to snap the hell out of it.

He thought they should stay together and
work through their differences. That's what a
normal couple who loved each other would do.
She didn't cry for long. After a sip of wine
and some time to relax, she slowly regained
control of her emotions. "I don't like to see
you cry. What can I do to make this right?"
"This is not like you. You're not the person I
expected to have dinner with. Why are you
being overly nice to me?"
"Well, I don't want to argue anymore. I want
to talk, listen to you."
The waiter was walking toward them, carrying a
large, round wooden tray with dinner. He
placed it on a tray stand near the table and
sat her plate down first. This guy is not
going to give up, she thought. He smiled a
little as he laid it down in front of her on
the table. He quickly gave her boyfriend his
plate and asked, "Will you need anything
else?" They both shook their heads to say no
and the waiter left. The food was delicious.
Seafood was her favorite kind of food to eat.
He didn't care much for fish. Steam released
from his chicken. As he cut into with a knife
and stabbed it with a fork it was juicy and
tender. They ate in silence for a short time.
It was masked by the noise of traffic on a
busy street. People walked by the area where
they were seated. A couple holding hands
strolled by and this made Iris feel insecure.
They used to hold hands just like them. She
thought of the beginning of their relationship
and compared things that happened now to
things that happened when they first met. He
was a different person back then and so was
she. "I think we should end things in a civil

manner." He stopped chewing and looked up from his plate. "Why do you want to end what we have?" He chewed the food still in his mouth. "Am I that terrible? I've done everything to help you with the bakery and I buy you anything you want. Why are you turning your back on me? On us?" She kept her eyes locked on his as he glared at her while he spoke. She could tell from the shakiness in the tone of his voice that he meant everything he said. "We've been—" She interrupted him in mid-sentence. "We've grown apart. I'm willing to leave the apartment if you don't want to." He was speechless after this and interested in finishing his meal. Silence was best for now. The fact that she would move out as if everything that transpired between them didn't matter at all, hurt.

He was also furious with himself for loving her so much. *Why did it have to end?* He imagined what she would do if he threw the dinner plate on the ground, snatched the entire table setting off, and let it fall there too. Iris would probably call the police. Reacting off pure emotion didn't seem to work anyway, especially a moment ago when he tried expressing how he felt they should work it out. He'd never been a quitter, but part of him was ready to wave the white flag and be with done with her altogether. *Who is he?* Relieved to have shared exactly what was on her mind, now she ate her dinner in peace.

The waiter came back. He could tell their date was an unpleasant one. He offered a dessert menu, but she didn't want any dessert. Steve ordered a slice of chocolate mousse cake. *Oh, great now I have to sit here longer with him.* He just wanted something sweet since emotions between them were sour. Each morsel

of cake made him feel a bit better. Josh
refilled her glass with wine. She sipped it.
"I think I'll stay in a hotel tonight."
"That's ridiculous." He frowned. "I won't
bother you. You can just sleep in our bed and
I'll take the sofa."
She liked this idea, although she didn't like
the fact that he was in control and she
allowed it. She imagined flinging the rest of
her wine at him. She was bitter with him for
trying to be the man she needed him to be
years ago.

THE PAST

Iris was ecstatic to go apartment hunting with Steve. They looked at several places before they made a final decision. This is how they always did things. They communicated well, considered each other's opinion and feelings about the type of grocery in the fridge, who would pay certain bills, where they would go for entertainment or dining. They had a perfect relationship. The distance between them started when he spent more time at work. Stressful, long hours as an accountant were demanding of his time. He hung out more with his buddies from college instead of being with her. One of his friends, a tall husky guy, was a jerk. He could easily convince Steve to go to the bar or to his house to hang out after work. Ron was a bachelor. He considered himself a ladies man. He bragged about never settling down with one woman. He claimed that relationships stifled freedom and kept a person from doing whatever he wanted to do in life. He liked having several different women to choose from.

Steve was the loyal type, but she worried that his friend would influence him to cheat. One day on a Saturday afternoon she tried to talk him out of hanging with his friends. She wanted him to stay with her so that they could go see a movie and then afterwards grab food to eat. He got upset with her and refused to cancel his plans with the guys. They had a shouting match, faulting each other about his insensitivity and her selfishness. The blame escalated into one of their worst arguments. They traded insults and called each other terrible names. She spent that Saturday alone. She went to the movies, did some shopping, and picked up Chinese food. She didn't expect to eat alone. He didn't come home until the next morning. He claimed after drinking he fell asleep at Ron's place. He didn't bother to apologize for not calling to let her know that he was safe and that he would spend the night there.

SOUR

Staring at her handsome boyfriend of five years she hoped to feel some kind of love. Too much pain. She wanted dinner to be over. He paid for it and walked her to her car. There was no affection. She watched him as he walked to his car. He had a great walk; a distinct bounce in his step. The wind lifted his thin black tie over his right shoulder. He felt good about dinner, although she tried to make it uncomfortable for him. He blamed her. None of this was his fault. At least he was trying, unlike her, to fix the relationship. He refused to accept her willingness to give up. Iris was relieved that she didn't have to ride home with him. Dead silence would have been worse than torture. There was more to be said between them. Nothing was settled at the restaurant.

Steve opened the car door, sat down, and loosened his neck tie. He undid the top button of his shirt. He lay back on the headrest and reclined the seat. He could smell her fragrance on his fingertips. He loved the way her skin smelled. He wondered exactly where things went wrong in their relationship. He had hopes of marrying Iris, but with everything falling apart it seemed there was a slim chance of this happening. Starting over with someone other than her was not something he anticipated. Tears streamed along his strong jawline. She had never seen him cry. He didn't wipe them. They needed to fall. The release was inevitable. No one other than his mother had seen him cry. He fell off his bike trying to leap over stacked cans in the alley behind his house. Friends dared him to do it. For years he kept his emotions chained to his soul. If he risked sharing them with her, he feared she would see him as a weak man.

When he was no longer in sight, Iris started her car. It wasn't too late in the evening and she regretted not having dessert. Ice cream would be the perfect indulgence for frustration and sadness. The ice cream would have gone well with his cake. She watched him be calm and nonchalant as he took each bite. There was a drug store a few miles from the restaurant. Someone was just pulling out of a parking space near it. Perfect timing. The meter had ten minutes left on it. She put enough money in, which gave her a total of twenty minutes in the space. She noticed a long line at the front register as she entered through automatic sliding doors. The store was busy with people buying various goods. She browsed the magazine aisle to pass the time. Others seemed to be in the store for the same reason.

She was in no hurry to be in the apartment with him. She squeezed between two readers standing near the magazine shelves. One was a short man of about fifty years old. He was heavy and had wiry grey hair. He looked Italian. The other was a pretty young woman who looked to be in her early twenties. She was reading a Cosmopolitan magazine. The older man was reading a PC World magazine. She thought he might be smart and an engineer. The young girl was probably a party girl into the latest fashion trends. She was either a college student or sales clerk in a department store Downtown.

Iris picked up a fitness magazine and flipped through the pages to find an article on the treadmill diet. She didn't need to go on a diet. She was in excellent shape and she ate healthy most of the time. When people learned that she was the owner of a bakery she noticed them sizing her up and wondering how she stayed slender as a baker. She ate her own cake, but moderation was her tactic to staying lean. Weight gain was never an issue for her. As a child she was thin and active. Her family did many things outdoors. They camped outdoors and took vacations that included hiking, swimming, and biking. In the frozen foods aisle, she took her time deciding on a flavor of ice cream. She loved vanilla, but it was out of stock. She liked to try new flavors and the caramel ice cream was one she had never tasted so she grabbed it. The coolness from the freezer gave her a slight chill.

The line had three people in it when she walked to the front register. A woman in a bright yellow blouse and floral scarf turned to her and said, "They should've opened the other register by now." She shook her head and waited for Iris to comment. She smiled at the woman and then looked away so that she wouldn't continue to talk to her. The caramel ice cream container softened in her palm. She told the cashier to keep the plastic bag. Ten minutes remained on the parking meter. Inside the car she opened the glove compartment and pulled out a plastic spoon. She ate the whole pint of caramel ice cream before leaving the parking space. She tried not to think of what Steve would say when she arrived home. She turned on the radio to a pop station and drove below the speed limit all the way to the apartment. She worried he would be awake and would want to continue the conversation from dinner. If he did, she planned on going to a hotel. This would prevent an argument which was unavoidable in the mental state she was in. Avalanched with a rush of mixed emotions. She didn't know whether to stop the car, get out, fall to her knees and cry or run screaming down the highway. Both ideas were completely irrational.

THE APARTMENT

She pulled in to the complex and parked her car in the space they paid sixty dollars for on a monthly basis. This was a reasonable fee considering that there were few to no available parking spaces on the street. She was grateful they had chosen to live in a building with covered parking. In the winter they didn't have to wipe off their cars like others in the neighborhood. They lived in a safe, quiet, upscale area in Lincoln Park. She couldn't afford to live there when she worked as an employee at the bakery. She had a modest income. Hard work for many years and ownership of the bakery improved her financial status. She believed in living within budgets. She never overspent for anything. If she found a coupon for something they needed in the apartment, she proudly used it. Iris took a deep breath and pushed the elevator button to her apartment floor. Outside the door, she swallowed hard. She put the key in the lock and turned it. Slowly she opened the door to reveal minimal contemporary furniture in the living room. No sign of Steve.

A low sigh of relief came out. She kicked off her shoes at the door and laid her red designer purse on a dark wooden stand near the coat rack on the wall. Gently she laid her keys there too. He didn't come out of the bedroom. She thought he must be in there asleep. She tiptoed through the living room and out the corner of her eye she saw him lying on the sofa under a blanket. The television was on, but the volume was low. He was sound asleep. The bottle of white wine on the coffee table was half empty. After a pity party alone, it helped him dose off. She was relieved that he was asleep. She went to the bedroom and slowly closed the door until she heard it click close. She undressed and took a hot shower. It had been a long day. In the shower, tears fell with the stream of water. *How can this be happening to me right now?* She needed to talk to someone. But there wasn't anyone she fully trusted with personal information. She had Carol and several other acquaintances that could have been close friends if Iris wasn't guarded. She believed that people listened to your troubles and then spread them to others. She thought of her employees at the bakery.

She could tell Tina who did a fairly good job of concealing her cuts which meant she was less likely to gossip. As she thought of the rest of her employees, she realized that she could confide in any of them. She had loyal workers, although they didn't spend a whole lot of time together outside the bakery, these were people she trusted with merchandise, money, and countless other duties in the business. Still she was afraid that if she shared anything about her failing relationship with Steve, they would worry and treat her differently. Mixing her personal life with the business was a bad idea. They might want to comfort or coach her through this rough phase in life. She didn't need any of them to think that she needed anything from anyone at any time. She was not about to appear as a weak boss. The shower was exactly what she needed to forget about her worries. She slid into a matching tank top and shorts set. No need for the sexy lingerie pieces that were in her drawer. She couldn't recall the last time she'd worn one for him. Sinking into their queen sized bed felt comfortable. Alone she had no concern for him at all. This was the kind of solitude she looked forward to and the kind of space she deserved.

In the middle of the night Steve awoke to a dark living room. He wondered if she came home until he noticed the bedroom door closed. When he slept in bed with her, the door remained open. He liked it this way. She seemed to be fine with it. He wondered how long he had been asleep until he saw the half empty bottle of wine he'd been drowning his sorrows in. The alcohol served its purpose. He used the light from his cell phone to see and poured himself another glass of wine. He drank alone in the dark and watched the bedroom door to see if she would come out. The apartment was quiet. Eventually in separate rooms they drifted into buried sleep.

The next morning arrived and he was greeted by a pounding headache. He wore the same dress shirt, pants, and socks from last night. The door was closed, which meant Iris would sleep in. The second bathroom was a nice perk, especially now that he didn't have to disturb her by showering in the master bedroom. The second bedroom was used as a guest room. When they decided on the apartment, he thought they wouldn't need more than one bedroom. She convinced him to consider family and friends who would occasionally visit and wish to stay over. She was right about this among other matters he didn't want to give her credit for.

He worked as an accountant for Joan, the former owner of the bakery. He did the payroll and balanced the accounts and kept track of the inventory for the bakery. This is how he and Iris met each other. The bakery did well and paid him a decent salary, but he had other aspirations. He wanted to work for a larger corporation. He shared this with her when they began dating and she encouraged him to pursue his dream. "If you don't try it, you will live to regret it," she said. They were on lunch break together. They had a slice of chocolate cake and a cup of coffee. He feared telling the owner because she was like family to him. She was good to him over the years. He received a large bonus every Thanksgiving and Christmas. The cake was also a nice benefit. He could help himself to some anytime he wanted it. She trusted him. He didn't want to disappoint her by leaving her. Following Iris' advice he spoke with Joan about leaving and she understood his reasoning. He continued to do the payroll and financial reports while he worked a new job at a top corporation in the area until she found another accountant to replace him.

When Joan died he was crushed by the news. The memory humbled him. In the guest bathroom, he realized that Iris had done many wonderful things for him in their relationship and he'd failed to acknowledge many of them. He showered and changed into casual clothes. He had treated her as if he didn't care about her for a few years if not more than that. The fact that he did this and still thought that things between them could be mended was absurd. He thought of Rene. For the first time he realized that he owed his girlfriend an apology. Had he ever done this? He should have apologized years ago. He would do it when she woke up to let her know that he was willing to do anything to save the relationship. Failure was not an option for him. When he landed the accountant position, he had to work his way up from entry level as an assistant accountant to the position he now held as a senior executive accountant. He made more money than he needed. He was an expert at handling money. He could pinpoint within minutes when something was off with any financial data. On the job he examined numbers and figures like a scientist. Everything had to align with imports and exports.

One year he noticed a significant gap in the company's financial gains. He had a hunch on what might have occurred, but he needed solid proof of the embezzlement before he took the news to the boss. He was an assistant working at ground level. If he was wrong, he'd be fired on the spot. His promotion came when he showed the senior analysts the paperwork to prove that someone had been stealing money from the company in small increments each week. The job was and still is demanding of his time. He enjoys it.

Steve made coffee for himself and Iris. He knew exactly how she liked her coffee. Black with two teaspoons of sugar. The aroma of coffee brewing lured her to open the bedroom door. "Morning, how did you sleep?" he said. "Fine, this is good coffee." Tension hovered as he watched her avoid eye contact. The bakery was closed on Sunday, but sometimes she would go in to check on orders or organize things for the next day. She didn't feel up to it today. "We need to talk," he said. "I know and I agree."
"Last night we didn't really settle this matter. This is difficult for me to handle. I love you and you're trying to dump me. I'm not alright with it."
"It's not easy for me either, but I don't see how we can get over this."

"I'm not asking you to get over it, but would you be willing to work through our differences?"

They were silent after this exchange and drank coffee. She looked at him seated across from her at the kitchen table. "I'm sorry for hurting you." She coughed, almost choked when she heard these words. He never apologized for anything that he had done or said to her. Tears began to well up in his eyes. She knew that he was sincere. It opened her heart to the idea of working things out. He blinked away his tears and finished his coffee. "Are you going out for a run today?" she said. "No, I thought we could spend the day together doing whatever you wanted to do." His cell phone rang in the living room. He didn't move to get it. This surprised her. Normally, he raced to get his phone. It didn't matter what he was doing when he heard it. He was always more concerned with taking the call than whatever was happening at the time. She thought his kind demeanor would only last for the day, but she appreciated it.

He hadn't been this kind to her in years. They argued almost every other day and it was overwhelming to be in the same space with someone who was a complete downer. She couldn't be down when she had a business to run with employees who depended on her. She had to keep her mood in check. No one dared to ask a question beyond the general one like *how are you doing?* She would always respond by saying that she was fine. She looked better than fine, her appearance was impeccable, but there was plenty wrong underneath the surface of a beautiful, calm face. She sat her mug on the table and crossed one leg over the other one. "Well, I'd like to go to the museum.

There's a new art exhibit I'd like to see. How do you feel about this?" she said. "I think it's a great idea. We haven't done that in a long time," he said.

THE DATE PART 1

The next morning both were in a pleasant mood. "I just have to shower and get dressed," she said. "Alright, I'm going to pick up a newspaper from the corner market. Do you want anything from there?" he said. "No, I don't want anything." Before leaving the kitchen, he kissed her on the cheek. She thought of how wonderful this would be if it continued. She had little faith that he would remain nice. In the shower, she washed her hair. She decided to let her naturally curly hair show today. Normally, she straightened it because Steve liked it this way. She hadn't been to the salon for color in over six months. Her reflection revealed the face of a woman in need of a boost. Her hair color looked drab against smooth, clear skin. She dressed in white jeans and a pale blue knit top. She grabbed nude sandals. As she buckled her sandals she wished her toenails were polished. She wondered if he would allow her to have some pampering done at the nail salon after their museum outing.

After a few sprays of fragrance she heard the key unlock the front door. "You look beautiful," he said. He didn't mention her hair. She wondered if he truly meant to give her the compliment, yet secretly wanted her to straighten her hair. "I need to change clothes and then we can head out," he said. She sat on the sofa to wait for him.

He drove without attempting any small talk with her. They listened to the radio on the way to the museum. His phone rang and he ignored it. *Why won't he answer it?* She paid for parking in the museum lot. While they walked toward the front doors of the building, he reached over and grabbed her hand. Holding

his hand felt awkward because this wasn't common for them. *What is he trying to prove here?* She got upset with him over this gesture and felt that she should address it now. She stopped walking and turned to face him.
"This doesn't feel right."
"What do you mean?"
"We haven't walked holding hands since our first date."
"Well, we have to start somewhere."
"If you think that you can just be nice to me for a day and then go back to ignoring me like you've been doing for years, we can end this right now." Steve shoved his hands in his pockets.
"Let's not start this again. If you're only focused on ending what we have, you can't even enjoy this moment."
"I never said that I wasn't enjoying this. Don't toy with me."
He knew this would lead to a huge argument and this was not how he wanted the day to go.
"Listen if holding your hand makes you uncomfortable, I won't do it. Should I wait until you invite me to touch you?" Iris didn't respond. "I really wanted to hold your hand and you. I want to be with you at this museum and anywhere else you may want to go. Can't you see that I'm trying here?"

As Steve gave his speech, she stared at him with her arms folded across her body. Her left foot was extended and her lips were pursed. He could tell that she didn't believe him and that she wanted to debate, be upset. He reached out and put his hands on the sides of her shoulders. "You know we can have a good time together. You have to be open to that."
He was right. She dropped the attitude since the museum was her suggestion, besides, she

wanted to see the art exhibit that everyone at the bakery was talking about. Some of her employees had invited her to go with them on a weekend day to see it, but she declined their invitation.

They entered the museum without holding hands. It was crowded with couples, families, and spectators. She noticed the couple standing in line in front of them. The man was carrying a baby girl and the woman standing next to him looked happy to be there. The baby girl could have been about eight months old. At that moment Iris wanted a child, although she wasn't a motherly type. She desired to have the same look in her eyes that the other woman had. She was in love and she envied her for that. She still loved her boyfriend of five years, but she didn't feel as if she could love him unconditionally like the woman in front of her who was now brushing aside the man's hair from his eyes. She stroked the back of his neck. Iris had thought of having a child and raising a son or daughter with Steve many years ago, but they were both busy trying to build their careers. She was skilled at baking and cooking. He was highly efficient with numbers. Their interest in success at work took precedence over everything else.

When she took over as the owner of the bakery, she asked if he would review the finances and help her balance the expenditures for supplies. Busy with his new position, he refused to help her. She resented him for this. He put other people's needs before hers. The memory enraged her. Instantly she forgot about wanting to have a child with him. He took a call from a coworker, his bar hopping buddy from work. She didn't care. Slowly they inched forward in line. She looked around at the crowd to people watch. He told his buddy that he was at the museum and she wondered what rude remark he heard on the phone because he laughed at whatever was said to him right after he shared his whereabouts. The conversation between them shifted to accounting business. She noticed other people on their cell phones and they were engrossed in conversations. He ended the call by telling his buddy that he would see him at work tomorrow. Inside the building was chilly. She wished for a jacket. His arms around her would provide the kind of warmth she needed. She had no interest in being perceived as a perfect couple. They looked fantastic together. Two attractive people who were about to break up. "I'll get one of those maps so that we can find everything." She nodded and thought it was a good idea. She told herself to try and make the best of this situation.

They walked down a long, quiet corridor. Marble floors and columns were magnificent to gaze at. They stopped for a short time to admire an abstract painting of man in pain. He read the description aloud and she agreed with him when he shared that it was an interesting piece. The colors were bold and artfully positioned on canvas. The lines in the man's face showed him as a serious older person. The detail of the other colors brought out the expression of pain. Her mood shifted from being irritated and uncomfortable to pleasant. She was an emotional rollercoaster. Sometimes she would feel high and lifted about her life. Other times she felt afraid, depressed, and lonely. Those feelings were the ultimate low for Iris. It was often difficult for her to avoid them.

She felt hot and moist. Wetness swelled above her brows then she felt a cool trickle of it glide down her spine. It was happening again. She was on the verge of having a panic attack. What would she do now? She couldn't let him know that this was happening to her. The mere thought of him knowing this secret she'd kept hidden from him for over a year would be devastating to her ego and embarrassing to reveal. He would think she was crazy. She tried to breathe deeply without exposing that she was struggling to keep her senses in order. "I need to go to the bathroom."

"Ok, I saw one near the front entrance when we were standing in that ridiculously long line." Her body temperature rose. She feared Steve would notice the perspiration, which was now streaming even more under her tight blue knit top.
She regretted her choice in fashion, but there was nothing she could do about it. She had to get away from him now before he detected the problem she was having. She couldn't handle the line of questioning that would surely ensue if he thought something was physically wrong with her. Luckily, he was distracted by other museumgoers and the gigantic, spiral metal art display in the center of the section where they stood. She resisted the urge to pant in front of him. "I--I remember where it is. I won't be long."
"That's fine. I'll stay in this area until you return." His hands were in his pockets. He was pressing the ignore button while his cell phone vibrated for an incoming call. He had an idea of who it might be on the other end. He wasn't going to risk answering it while they were trying to have a pleasant time. She

walked backwards away from Steve until he turned to walk toward the metal art on display. He was easily distracted and she liked this about him now because it was just what she needed from him to keep her secret. She raced toward the entrance of the museum, hoping no one noticed huge sweat stains spread under her armpits. Her vision blurred as she approached the bathroom. People looked like they were tilted instead of standing upright. She felt weak as if she would faint. She leaned into the stall to balance herself. "Are you alright?" A middle aged Chinese woman came into view when her vision returned to normal. She was starting to cool off. The panic attack was a short one. The adrenaline rush from her condition almost being exposed must have helped. "I'm fine and thank you." The woman stared at her for a moment and then wet a paper towel. "Here take this, you're red. Are you sure that you're alright? I'd be happy to get security for you." She used the wet paper towel to blot her forehead. "No, that won't be necessary."

Realizing there was nothing she could do for Iris, the woman left the bathroom. Alone she looked at her reflection in the mirror. Her cheeks and neck were bright red like she was sunburned. She pressed the cool paper towel against her neck and took deep breaths. *How am I going to hide this?* The sweat stains in the armpits of her top were noticeable. She turned on the hand dryer, but the spout was stationary. She removed her top and placed it under the dryer, moving it back and forth until it was mostly dry. She had to hurry otherwise Steve would get suspicious and come looking for her. She tried to figure out what triggered the panic attack. She had them as often as three times a week. When one came on, she usually knew the reason for it. This time it was different. She was just standing with him looking at artwork. *Was it the expression of the man in the piece? Or was it the couple with the baby girl who looked so happy in love?* She didn't know how to explain it, but this was something she had to speak to her therapist about.

Another secret her boyfriend was unaware of. She had been going to a psychiatrist for three years. She began seeing Dr. Morgan when she experienced panic attacks for the first time in her life. She didn't know what was happening to her. She felt hot all over and anxious. She had been shopping for items for the bakery. The symptoms of the panic attack came over her out of nowhere. She thought she was dying. The mall security called for an ambulance and it took her to the emergency room. The doctor on duty was extremely busy that day. He was preoccupied with more severe matters of patients with critical injuries. He didn't take the time to diagnose her symptoms or even discuss her family's health history. He told her that it was probably a result of dehydration. She took his advice to drink more water and to minimize the amount of exercise she was doing per week to three to four days instead of six days. The next time the panic attack occurred, she knew that it had nothing to do with a lack of water and over exercising.

When it happened, Iris was alone in her office. Like the first time, she felt the same heat rise inside her body, her palms and forehead became sweaty and she felt extremely dizzy. *What's wrong? Do you need me to drive you to the hospital? Are you alright?* Their words all seemed to mesh together. It was all too much for her. She said no to them and then she left the bakery in a hurry. Her employees were concerned. It was short notice, but she had to call her personal doctor. On the way there in the car she dialed the number and raced through a few turning red traffic lights before she crossed the intersection. In the lobby, she tried to look calm. She believed that everyone seated near her could tell that she was panicked. Her blouse clung to her body. It was cold and wet. *This is embarrassing, especially when strangers can see you have a problem. Stop looking at me.*

The doctor told her that she had a panic attack, her heart sunk. "What causes this?" Dr. Sherwood explained that they stem from having major anxiety over something. It could be anything that causes high levels of anxiety. They come out of nowhere and some people have repeat episodes. She was one of those people. He prescribed Xandal to help her cope. She took them once and the pills made her feel lethargic and clueless. She never took them again, but did take Dr. Sherwood's recommendation to give his colleague Dr. Morgan, who was a good therapist, a call. Steve could never know about her going to therapy. He would definitely think she was crazy. He would use it against her, call her a liar, and blame her for their break up.

Iris worried that she might have spent too much time in the bathroom at the museum. Her top was dry and her nerves were calm. She walked back to the spot where he was waiting for her. He smiled at her. She returned the gesture trying to avoid too much eye contact with him. "Are you ready to see that new art exhibit you were talking about?"

"Yes, which way should we go?" He opened the museum map and they both looked at it. He was much better at reading it than she was. He pointed to the location and they began to walk there. "I could use something cold to drink."
"There's a kiosk where we can buy lemonade near the exhibit. Would you like to stop there?"
"I would, I'm very thirsty." His phone vibrated in his pants pocket again and this time he answered. She didn't care. It took his attention away from her. She guessed it was someone from work because his tone and dialogue was all business. He told the caller he was at the museum. She was the woman Steve had been seeing off and on for the past year. He was cheating on his girlfriend, although he had no intention of leaving her for Rene. He loved Iris. Rene was someone he shared time with when things were rough at home. She was someone he would talk to. Someone to complain to about his frustrations in his relationship. They were friends and nothing more than that.

THE DATE PART 2

He had never been intimate with Rene. There were a few moments when kisses almost led to more, but he stopped her from unbuttoning his shirt. She knew that he loved his girlfriend. She hoped Steve would realize that he was better off with her. She would do anything to make him the happiest man alive. When he told her he was at the museum, she ignored it. She asked if they could hang out again. She suggested they meet for lunch one day in the week. He said that he would get back to her with the date so that they could discuss the paper work for setting up a new account. She overlooked the cover-up. He pretended that she was a potential client he would be doing business for and she knew that he was lying so that his girlfriend wouldn't discover the truth. Rene envied her, but she didn't care that he was deceitful to his girlfriend. She believed he would never be this way with her. She wouldn't give him a reason to. She was overzealous about her involvement with Steve. He knew that he had to straighten things out with her; otherwise she would cause trouble for him while he was trying to patch things up with Iris.

He abruptly ended the call and tried to put the matter out of his mind. They stopped for lemonade. The drink was refreshing and tangy with just the right amount of sweetness. He paid for the drinks and he thought of how they always did things like that for each other. When they went out to places, they split the cost. They didn't argue about who would pay for something. Money was never a taboo topic or an issue for them. Both had plenty of it. They worked hard and managed how they spent it. They had separate bank accounts for personal spending. They opened a joint account to which each contributed biweekly funds. They used that money for bills, dining out, and entertainment.

Finally, they made it to the art exhibit. He was surprised to see so many people were interested in looking at it. They couldn't get a clear view of the display from where they were standing so they tried moving to the other side in hopes of squeezing in between the crowd to see what all the hype was over. They were both amazed by what they saw. It was a rock encased in glass. There were two floor lights beaming on it. In a whisper voice he said, "What's so special about this rock?" "It's supposed to be the oldest stone of its kind. The stone is dated 3000 BC" Now he was fascinated, initially he thought it was an ordinary hunk of limestone that had been buffed and labeled as ancient. The museum had the area roped off so that everyone had to stand behind it. He wanted to move beyond the ropes so that he could really see the detail of the rock. There was no chance of that, especially with the stone being heavily guarded by four armed men. There was one standing at each corner inside the roped area. Who would want to steal a rock or stone from a prehistoric age baffled him. He was enjoying his time at the museum with Iris. He wished that they had this kind of fun all the time. Spending time with her made him recall how much he enjoyed her company.

They stared at that exhibit for over an hour just like the other spectators. He reached out to grab her hand and surprisingly this time she let him hold it without any hesitation or complaint. She felt his love. As they were walking toward the entrance to leave, she mentioned she had a taste for pasta. "How would you feel about making it at home?"

"We haven't cooked together in a long time. I'd like to do this." He drove to the market place near their apartment. She picked out angel hair pasta and he selected the sauce. "Should we have a baguette of French bread too?"

"Absolutely, it's so much better than frozen garlic bread." As they waited to check out, she thought it was impossible for them to continue having a pleasant day. They had spent almost the entire day together and now they were going to cook in the same kitchen. She paid for the groceries while he put them in plastic bags.

On the way home, they were silent in the car. He didn't bother to ask what her thoughts were. She stared out the window. She seemed to be in deep thought. *This feels right to be in the car in silence with him. All day he's been the perfect gentleman. Why do I still want out of this relationship? Something isn't right between us and it's been that way for over a year. I don't think things will ever be like they were when we first met. I've spent all this time with him and I truly don't know him. I should know everything about him, but I don't. What bothers me most is that I don't care to know everything.* She took a deep breath in and exhaled hard. *How did I get here? How will I ever tell him the truth about my panic attacks?* His phone ringing broke her thoughts. He didn't answer and she noticed he seemed a bit anxious about it. This was unlike him. "Why didn't you check to see who was calling?" He smiled and said, "I'd rather talk to you. Everyone else can wait."

She turned to continue looking out the window. He knew it was probably Rene calling again. It irritated him that she called back. He had to end it with her. If his girlfriend left him, it would be his entire fault. He couldn't live with that kind of regret. In many ways, he led Rene on, used her for someone to lean on while he and Iris were having problems. He knew that she was falling hard for him shortly after they began hanging out. They always met at the location if they went out for food. He never invited her to his apartment. When he needed comfort and company, she was always there. She opened her door to him anytime he requested it. Rene was a great woman. She wasn't his girlfriend. He loved Iris more than he loved himself. He felt like he loved her more than she loved herself. It was obsessive the way he felt about her.

When they walked through their apartment door, they smelled a foul odor. It was the garbage. He forgot to take it out before they left for the museum. Steve tied and grabbed the bag then tossed it in the dumpster behind the building. The owners of the complex did a fairly decent job of upkeep with the grounds. They paid reasonable rent. They both felt safe where they lived and this was something they wanted when they were searching for an apartment together. Iris tried to remember if he asked her to move in with him or if it was the other way around. She was nervous about asking him this detail from their past history together, but she really couldn't remember and thought it was best if he told her how they came to live together. She put a large pot of water on the stove to boil. While he spoke, she was quiet. "We had been dating for over six months. You and I both worked at the bakery. Your lease was about to end the following month and over cake and tea I asked if you wanted to move in with me."

"Did I say yes right away?"

"No, you told me the next day at work. I didn't mind the wait; somehow I knew you would agree to do so." He smiled as he opened the package of pasta. She put it in the water, which was rapidly boiling. He began working on the sauce. "Al Dente for you?" She said it with an accent and giggled. He laughed too. They understood each other's jokes. While the food was cooking she set the plates and silverware on the table. He left the kitchen to change into comfortable clothing and later she did the same. This moment, cooking with him in the kitchen, felt loving as if they had no troubles.

While Steve was in the bathroom changing into a t-shirt and shorts he sent Rene a quick text message. "Hi Rene, now is not a good time for us to talk, but I want to clear up a few things." On impulse Rene called him as soon as she read the message. She wanted to know what he meant by clearing up things. She suspected he was going to end things with her. She was unhappy about it. She felt slighted by his dismissive attitude. For the first time since she had been with him, she felt used. She wasn't going to be tossed aside like trash. She spent many nights listening to Steve gripe about his girlfriend and how bad things were at home. She rubbed his shoulders and then there was the kiss. It was gentle and intimate. It made her feel incredible. She believed he shared her sentiment. She felt close to him that night her lips pressed against his. *Why would he end things now?* She had no intention of revealing their secret.

She wanted to continue building their friendship. She hoped that he would eventually leave his girlfriend so they could be together. She wouldn't admit it to anyone, but she was obsessed with him. She'd never felt this way about any man in her life. He declined the call and figured it was best to turn his phone off. He worried a little that he would miss important calls this evening, but Rene was being persistent and stubborn. This angered him. He wanted to let her down easy. He realized he would have to be stern with her.

In the kitchen, Iris was seated at the table. He was ready to enjoy the pasta they'd prepared together. They ate and talked about things they saw at the museum.

"I liked that huge metal display in the middle of the museum. It was one of kind, don't you think so?"

"I do and I feel that's what curators look for when they have a new item to reveal to people."

"I really didn't think you would ever want to go to the museum with me."

"Are you kidding, me? As a child, I enjoyed going to the museum all the time. Everything was enormous to me. I was a short boy for a long time while growing up. Then one summer I grew like a weed. Instantly, I was taller and everyone at my school noticed it to."

"You've never shared this with me."

"It's funny, I know. I want to share everything with you." He grabbed her hand. She didn't pull away. She cried and said, "How did we get here? You've been so wonderful today. You've done everything I've asked of you and you don't seem like yourself even now." He listened and kept hold of her hand. "Where's the mean guy who barely said more than two words in passing to me each day? For over a year you've been a stranger to me."

He knew that she needed to get those emotions out. They had been pinned up for so long. Dinner was mostly gone. He let go of her hand, got up for a tissue to wipe her tears. He didn't like to see her cry and he knew how she felt. He had been a jerk. He felt terrible about it. He wondered if he should confess that he had been seeing another woman. No, this would make matters worse between them. Telling her would only serve his ego and ease his conscious of deception. Revealing the truth wouldn't do anything for her feelings, except crush them, make her feel inadequate. Iris was the perfect woman for him. "I'm sorry that I've hurt you so much." He said this while wiping tears from her face, which was a little red. "I'll clean the dishes and then pour us some wine. Why don't you relax for a bit?" This was perfect advice. She followed it. Wearing cut-off denim shorts and a loose pink fleece top, she grabbed the remote lying on the sofa. Television, although unappealing to her mood right now, provided the distraction she needed to get through this evening. She was glad the week was over. Steve scraped the leftover food from the plates into the trash can. They had a garbage disposal. It was hardly put to use.

He stacked dishes next to the sink then he turned the faucet on and adjusted the temperature of the water. It had to be just right. The water couldn't be scalding hot or lukewarm so somewhere in between those temperatures was perfect for him. He put the stopper in and squeezed a long squirt of dish liquid into the water. He watched the suds

form a white bubbly mound on top of the water.
He immersed three fingers of his right hand
into the water to distribute the suds evenly
around it as it filled the kitchen sink. It
was a large, double stainless steel,
restaurant style sink. He favored stainless
steel appliances. The stove and refrigerator
matched it. When the sink was mostly filled
with water, he turned off the faucet and
submerged each dish individually and then he
dropped the silverware in it. He washed those
items first and placed the sudsy dishes on the
other side of the sink without any water. He
washed the larger pot that held the pasta
first then the smaller pot that he used to
cook the sauce. He removed the stopper and
watched the water spiral down the drain. They
didn't have to pay for water so he didn't mind
it running while he rinsed the dishes.

He picked up each dish and rinsed it. He
grabbed the silverware and rinsed them. There
were suds lagging behind so he turned the
faucet back on to get rid of them. He mixed
the suds with running water and then scooted
the suds down the drain. He placed them on a
cloth that lay on top of the counter. He
rinsed the pots separately and then let them
sit for under a minute in the sink. He
retrieved the dry dish towel from the hook in
the lower cabinet next to the stove and dried
the two pots one at a time. He placed them on
top of the stove. He wiped the remaining
wetness from his hands with the same towel.
This was his process every single time he
washed the dishes. She had one too. She was
grateful that he offered to do the dishes. In
the upper cabinet near the refrigerator, he
removed two short wine glasses. The wine
cooler contained a variety of wines. He chose

a dry white wine and filled each glass almost to the rim.

He wanted to feel closer to Iris this evening and he hoped the wine would relax her. *Sex would be nice*. He handed her a glass and sat down beside her. "What are we watching?" "Not sure, I think it's a suspenseful crime movie." She extended one of her legs to lay her foot on the coffee table. She had beautiful legs. There were no scars or cellulite that most women her age worried about. She attributed her features to her family genes. She knew that he was watching her and wanted to touch her, she liked feeling his eyes roam over her body. She welcomed his adoration. She extended the other leg and crossed it over the other one on the coffee table. *Should I put my hand on her thigh and gently rub it? What's the worst thing that could happen?* He wanted her to initiate the first move. Their evening together was better than most nights, at least they were in the same room. He didn't mention her crying spell. She appreciated that he wasn't talking much at all. Sitting on the sofa next to the man she still loved deeply was all the comfort she needed at the moment.

They watched the movie on television until the wine was gone. He took the glasses and placed them on the kitchen counter. She stood up and removed the fleece sweatshirt. Underneath it was an off-white tank top. She walked toward the bedroom and he followed her. She removed her shorts and climbed into bed. He liked the way her panties fit, lifted to reveal her butt cheeks. He got in on the other side and wondered if things would go further. He waited for her to make a move. She didn't and he was fine with it. He was grateful to lie close to her, feel her warmth, and smell her skin. She liked that he didn't try to force intimacy into their evening. The day went so smoothly and now the evening matched it.

THE OTHER WOMAN

The next day, sunrise woke him first. Iris was sound asleep. He pulled the comforter back on his side. Then he carefully eased his left foot onto the floor, trying not to shake the mattress too much. He sat straight up in bed and put the other foot down. Slowly he rose off the bed and tip-toed over a hardwood floor to the guest bathroom. He pulled on a tank top he left there from another night. Luckily, a pair of worn socks was in there too. Steve often left items of clothing lying around the apartment. She picked up after him. As he tied his gym shoes, he worried about Rene being in his life. A good run would help ease the stress.

Outside he inhaled a cool gust of wind. Before he began jogging, he turned on his phone. He noticed ten missed calls from Rene. He was infuriated by her repeated attempts to get in touch with him. She left only one voice message: *I don't understand why you're not answering my calls. I haven't done anything wrong. We need to talk and you said that you would get back to me. Well, when? How long do I have to wait? Listen, I know you have a ton of pressure on you at the moment and I'm not trying to add to this, but I can't live without you. I don't even care about her. The way I feel about you keeps me awake at night. Were all the times we've shared for nothing? I know that you care about me. You're just trying to do what feels right. Honestly, I feel disappointed. Will you please talk to me? I won't take no for an answer. I deserve more than that. Please talk to me so that we can work this out.*

Rene talked until time ran out. He dragged the number one indicating her message was on his phone to the garbage icon at the bottom of the unlocked screen. *Why bother listening to it?* She had already made it clear that she wanted to speak to him. He told her that he would contact her. That should have been enough. Her persistence annoyed him and it showed a different side of who she really was. She would have to wait whether she liked it or not. Speaking to her wasn't a priority. The only issue that concerned him was making things right in his relationship with his girlfriend. Rene was completely out of line. He didn't owe her anything because he hadn't made any promises to her. From the start of their involvement she knew that he was committed to Iris. He placed his phone in his right pocket and zipped it. He liked workout wear that was functional. The zip up pocket would ensure that he wouldn't lose his money while he ran.

He jogged slowly at first to warm up his body. After a few blocks, he listened to music on his iPod. The sounds of Hip-Hop beats made him pick up the pace as he moved into a full out sprint. He was a good runner. He positioned his body in perfect form as he ran faster. Heel to toe was his method each time his feet hit the pavement. *Comfortable clothing is also essential. When you begin to perspire, breathable clothing is the best option to have on your body.* He told Iris this while they shopped for workout gear. She listened to his advice because he was in excellent shape. She loved to hear him talk about anything when things were perfect between them.

When he broke out into a fast sprint, he turned off the music but left the ear buds in so that he could listen to his breathing.

Pushing himself to run harder and faster. His legs burned and he enjoyed it. He thought of Iris. She was the one who gave him an important push in life when he needed it most. She supported his decision. Threatening to end their relationship encouraged him to take a closer look at himself and how he had taken her for granted. He expected her to tolerate everything he said or did. On many occasions she had no voice. Her opinion didn't matter. He made certain that she was aware of this. But she didn't complain about it.

When Iris woke, he was already gone. She knew exactly where he was. His actions were the same for years. He was so predictable. He went out for a run five days a week. Being fit was as important as accounting was to him. She noticed that he'd left the wine glasses out from the previous night. They needed to be washed. She couldn't resist the urge to urine. Quickly she walked to the guest bathroom. While seated on the toilet, she had to blow her nose. As she finished, she was about to throw away balled up tissue and noticed a few crumpled receipts in the trash.

A weird feeling came over her. One of the receipts had the name of the restaurant they went to the other night. But the other receipt was from Jimmy's Crab Palace. They had never been their together. When she opened it, the details showed Steve had dinner there a week ago. Two entrees and a bottle of expensive red wine were ordered. This made her uncomfortable. She thought about what was happening in their lives at that time and realized that the night the receipt was dated was the same night he said he'd work late at the office. The time on the receipt was after ten in the evening. Her heart sunk. She took a deep breath in and slowly exhaled. He lied to her. *But why would he do this?* She threw the other receipt back into the garbage can, but kept the one she was suspicious about. She didn't know how to approach him about the matter.

This was something else she had to share with her therapist. Now was the perfect time to call and schedule an emergency appointment with Dr. Morgan. As a regular in the office, she had no problem booking the appointment. She had a weekly appointment scheduled before going to the bakery, but she needed to speak with her therapist sooner than this. Iris trusted Dr. Morgan as an unbiased listener who could help her figure out how to handle the problems in her life. She was eager for the morning appointment.

In the meantime, she had to appear as if everything was normal between her and her boyfriend. No sooner than she thought this, she heard the key in the front door click to unlock it. Steve was sweaty and hyped from his run. She heard music blaring from his ear buds. Loudly he asked, "Would you make me a cup of coffee?" Then he kissed her on the cheek. She rolled her eyes and wiped the wetness off her cheek. When he removed his wet t-shirt, he almost tossed it on the floor as he walked to the bedroom. He held it until he saw the hamper.

He didn't notice Iris watching him. She followed him into the bedroom, glaring at him as he undressed. He kicked off his gym shoes and then in one swoop pulled off his boxers and jogging pants. The luster of his naked body made her tingle inside. She wanted to join him in the shower, let his strong hands lather and touch her. At that moment she felt his lips on hers. They kissed lovingly, panted while touching, and both were aroused standing in the bedroom until she pulled away from him. The look in her eyes showed that she wasn't ready to open her heart to him again. She walked to the living room and he took a cool shower. When he came out, she was dressed casually and said, "I'm going to the bakery for a few hours." He knew that meant she would stay until closing time. He didn't want her to go, but he gave her the impression that he was fine with it.

TINA AND IRIS

She enjoyed being at the bakery on Sundays to manage the business. She also liked to assist employees in any way that she could. Soon the bakery would enter its busiest season. The holidays meant long hours baking specialized cakes for office parties and family gatherings. Everyone worked hard and sometimes around the clock to make certain that orders didn't get backed up. It was busier than usual at the bakery so no one noticed her mood. Iris felt low. But more than this she felt confused. *Who had Steve gone to dinner with at Jimmy's Crab Palace?* He was careless to leave the receipt in the trash can. She wanted to believe that there was a reasonable explanation for it, but in her heart she knew that he was covering something up. This was the only thing she could focus on while at the bakery.

Normally, the routine of gathering ingredients for cake recipes was enough distraction from her thoughts. This wasn't working out today. Tina asked if she could speak with her in private before she left. Iris didn't have the heart to deny her another chance to vent. She wanted to tell her no because she didn't feel like being bothered with another woman's problems. She worried that Tina might cut herself if she didn't listen to her. She avoided the conversation until the end of the day. Everyone else was gone for the day. She turned off the open sign and the lights in the store front. They were alone. Tina finished counting the money in the register and placed it in a blue vinyl pouch. After leaving the bakery Iris would make the bank drop. Tina began the conversation. "How are you today? You seem a little down." She wondered what made her recognize her true feelings. She tried best to conceal how upset she was with her boyfriend. "I'm fine. I just have a lot on my mind."

"Do you want to talk about it?"

Tina closed the cash register and walked toward Iris who was standing near a cake decorating table. She placed a hand on her bosses shoulder. "I'm here for you. You've done so much to help me. How could I give you anything less than the same in return?" They smiled. Locked in Tina's gaze, she knew her words were sincere. She felt as if she could share some of her relationship blues. Iris leaned on the table. "My boyfriend and I are trying to mend our relationship. He wants to stay together and I don't anymore."

"Oh no, this is terrible. I'm sorry you're going through this. How long have you been with him?"

"Five years. We live together and the tension between us at our place is difficult at times."

"I'm sure it is." Iris stood straight and walked into her office to get her belongings. Tina followed her. "Have you ever thought about going to couples counseling?" Iris shook her head to say no. She had considered this method early in the relationship when things between them seemed to be going in a negative direction. She didn't want to disclose too much personal information to her employee. Tina was a sweet girl, but she wasn't a close friend. She worried the others might find out what they'd discussed and then the rumors in the bakery would start. She didn't want to make anyone else responsible for her problems. She changed the subject to what was going on in Tina's life. "How are things with you and your fiancé?" This worked perfectly and she took the bait. "Things aren't going so well for us either. I thought about what you said when we last spoke. I thought I could live the rest of my life being by his side, but the prenuptial agreement is ridiculous. I'm never going to sign it. It's caused him to postpone the wedding."

Iris was shocked by the news. She never thought she would have the courage to speak up for herself and tell her fiancé how she really felt about the prenup. She embraced her with a tight hug for a long time. As Iris slowly released her arms from around Tina, she felt a soft kiss on her neck and then another one on her cheek. *What's happening here?* Tina traced her bosses face with more kisses. Iris was frozen in place. They were standing near the desk. She thought of doing or saying something to stop Tina's kisses, but she didn't know what to do or say in that moment. When she felt Tina's lips press against hers, a warm sensation surged through her body and then she realized that she wanted more of those kisses. Kisses. Those were tender and loving. Kisses. Those were sensual and wet. She wanted them from Steve. Her heart ached. Her eyes welled up with tears. Tina held her face between the palms of her hands and kissed Iris on the tip of her nose. "You deserve better from a man." She tried to blink away her tears before they fell. Tina gave her a tissue.

They left the bakery in silence. As Iris locked the door, she said "Have a good evening and safe drive home." They got in their cars and drove off. Tina ignored a call from her fiancé and this made her feel empowered. Iris pushed thoughts of what happened with Tina out of her mind. She called Steve to ask if he wanted anything from the drug store. *I've just kissed a woman. It's nothing.* He didn't answer.

STEVE AND RENE

He was on the phone with Rene. She pleaded with him to reconsider ending their interaction. "I don't feel comfortable continuing to see you. I love Iris and if she ever found out about me spending time with you, she would leave me for good. You have to understand that the thought of this kills me." "What am I to you? Do you think that you can just mistreat me as if I don't have feelings?" "I never said that."

"I care about you and I don't understand how you can say this is over. You told me you cared about me too. I believe that somewhere in your heart you still do." Steve put a hand over his eyes as he held the phone. "Listen, Rene I don't owe you anything. But at least I'm giving you the truth. I need you to respect what I'm telling you and be mature about this situation." She was silent so he ended the call. He hoped the conversation would be a final one. He thought she really needed to get over her feelings. He was completely turned off by her desperation and persistence. He felt slightly bad about kissing her, but that was all they did. *How could she become so attached to me?* They only kissed a few times. He didn't take it any further than that.

She sighed and stared at her phone after he hung up. She was upset that he didn't say goodbye to her. He sat on the sofa staring at the television and reflected on the first time he kissed Rene. They were at her place. They often went there, especially after having dinner. In most cases they merely talked about their day and jobs. The night of the first kiss was unlike any other one he spent with her. Earlier that day he had an argument with

Iris and needed some company. He looked to
Rene for that and he genuinely enjoyed being
around her. She was a beautiful woman. She
could have any man of her choice. She told him
once that she always got involved with men who
were either disinterested in or unavailable
for a committed relationship. She felt that
all the good guys were taken.

Meeting a man that she was attracted to
always seemed to turn out this way. She and
the guy would get to know each other and then
the guy would reveal that he wasn't single or
didn't want to be tied down. She was always
disappointed by the same scenario. Her last
relationship had been with a married man. They
were together for three years. She believed
that he was eventually going to leave his wife
for her. She felt like a gullible idiot for
being led on by him for so long. Steve felt
empathy for her troubles with men. They talked
and became quite comfortable with each other
that night. They were drinking wine. Her touch
aroused him. He wanted to take things further
with Rene. She was a great kisser. Her lips
were soft and the warmth of her tongue, the
wetness of her mouth aroused him more. She
helped him lift off her blouse. He kissed and
grabbed her breasts. An image of his
girlfriend came to mind and he pulled back
from her. She wanted to continue. She didn't
care that he wasn't a single man. This was a
trend she couldn't break free of, giving in to
this moment between them felt right. He turned
cold. Topless she watched as he grabbed his
wallet and keys. He left her place and slept
over Ron's house.

The other time he kissed Rene was when
they were leaving a restaurant. On the way to
his car, they were holding hands. He didn't

feel strange about walking the streets with another woman while Iris was home alone. He had a tremendous ego. He felt that he could do whatever he wanted and be with whomever he wanted. He and his girlfriend had no intimacy at this point in their relationship. It bothered him a great deal, but he was turned off by her bad attitude. He didn't even bother to make any moves to rekindle the physical aspect of their relationship. Rene smelled like spring that evening. She also made him feel like he mattered. He missed having that feeling of being desired by his counterpart. Rene's backside was pressed against the passenger side of his car. Her long black straight hair lifted in the breeze. He pressed his body against hers and kissed her aggressively. For a second time he was ready to go all the way with her. His hand was underneath her dress, between her thighs. He wanted to take her right there in the parking lot.

He received a text from Iris. She asked him to stop at the store for a gallon of water. She said they were all out and that he would need it for his morning run. Guilt surged through his entire body. She was showing that she still cared about him and his interests. He would be pissed if there was no water in the fridge for him to drink before he went jogging. She knew this and it made him change his mind about going to Rene's place. He could tell by the glare she gave him when he told her the news that she was highly disappointed. She tried to appear understanding. She believed that if she remained patient with him he would have a change of heart about being in a dead relationship. This would mean that they could be together. She planned to make him happy. Now she wouldn't get that chance. When she thought of their phone conversation, Rene cried hysterically. She fell to her knees, agonizing over yet another failed involvement with a man. *What's wrong with me? I don't deserve this treatment.* She threw her cell phone across the living room floor and continued to cry and moan for hours. She looked pathetic lying on a carpeted floor crying over a man who clearly cared more for himself than her. She would need ample time to get past the incident.

THE APARTMENT

He waited for Iris to return home from the bakery. She would try being affectionate so that Steve wouldn't detect her suspicions. With her fingers and the back of her hand she wiped her mouth. Tina was wearing pink tinted lip-gloss. Iris grinned at the thought of the moment they shared in her office. She wanted to enter the apartment, ignore him, and go straight to bed. This would cause an argument. She had to avoid one. She wished it was the next morning and that she was already in her car on the way to see Dr. Morgan. As soon as she opened the door he was there to greet her. They embraced. "How was everything at the bakery?"

"Busy as usual. We have a ton of cake orders to fill." He took her purse and placed it on the table in the dining room. "Would you like something to eat? I ordered Chinese food."

"That sounds good, but I just want a small portion." He smiled and they walked in opposite directions. He went into the kitchen to warm food for her. She went into the bedroom to change clothes. She put on a grey sweatshirt and matching loose sweat pants. It was the least complimenting outfit she could find in the closet. If he found her attractive in it she would have to find another way to deflect his advances. A saucer with beef and broccoli over white rice was on the coffee table. He was on the sofa waiting for her to join him. "Thanks for the food. Did you eat already?"

"I did. I ate a little too much. I'm tired now." While she was eating, he lowered his body deeper into the sofa cushions. He searched the channel guide for a good movie to watch. There was nothing interesting on. He

90

left it on a reality cop show. She picked at
her food in silence. She was surprised that he
didn't try to touch her at all. He sat on the
sofa with his arms folded across his stomach.
He thought of the conversation with Rene. It
didn't go well. He wondered if Rene had tried
to contact him again. His cell phone was
turned off. The secrecy made him edgy. He
closed his eyes to relax. Hurriedly she ate
the food, crept to the kitchen, and washed her
plate and silverware. Steve fell asleep on the
sofa. Tonight she felt lucky. She didn't try
to wake him. She tiptoed to bed. Hours later
he climbed in bed next to her.

DR. MORGAN

The master bathroom had a double sink. It was large enough for them to get ready for work at the same time. Steve rose before her and began his morning ritual: aiming over the toilet, shaving, brushing his teeth, undressing, and finally hopping in the shower. Her routine was similar to his except that after brushing her teeth she went into the kitchen to make lunch for the day. She never made him lunch. He liked to go out for food. It gave him a break from the office. She thought he wasted too much money on eating out. His argument was that he could spend his money how he pleased; besides, he made healthy choices. After she prepared her lunch, she returned to the bedroom and laid out clothes for work. She dressed in business casual attire some days and on other days she dressed like a runway model in London. Her expensive taste for designer clothing and accessories was noted by everyone at the bakery. Normally he was finished in the shower by the time she had her outfit together.

Steve lingered awhile this morning and she was slightly thrown off by his actions. She was not in the mood to join him in the shower. But she enjoyed admiring his strong physique in the mirror. The steam from the shower partially covered his reflection. She wore a loosely tied, pink silk robe with a few embroidered flowers on it. While nude he dried himself off, greeted her and kissed her on the forehead, and then walked into the bedroom to get dressed. She stood in the bathroom with her cleavage exposed. *Why didn't he try to take things further with me?* She was baffled by his avoidance. It made her even more suspicious that the person he took to dinner at Jimmy's Crab Palace was someone he didn't want her to know anything about. Quickly, they both dressed. He made coffee and put it in a stainless steel travel mug. "Have a wonderful day at the bakery."

"Thanks. Enjoy adding figures." They kissed on the lips. It was the first time they had done this in months. Years of tension built up between them. Affection had become obsolete. When the door closed behind him, she let out a sigh of relief. She checked her makeup in the mirror of the master bathroom. It was flawless. She liked wearing light makeup to enhance her features and not to cover them up. She wore a tailored, tan pants suit with a silk, pastel pink blouse. It had a scoop neckline. It was soft against her skin. It made her feel beautiful. She slipped on a pair of nude patent leather pumps. Her purse matched the shoes. Ready to go see Dr. Morgan, she grabbed her lunch from the kitchen counter and walked out the door. She had an hour before her appointment. She called the office to confirm she would be there. Next, she called Kevin. He was the team leader who handled the business when she was absent. She was rarely absent from the bakery. He wanted to know was everything alright with her and she told him she was fine and that she would be in later. She lied. She only said it so that he wouldn't probe further with questions.

A few clients were waiting in the office to see Dr. Morgan. Iris was calm. She sat in the seat closest to the wall and waited patiently for her name to be called. The doctor had just finished a session with a couple on the verge of a breakup. When they came out, both looked frustrated and sad. They were an adorable looking couple. They reminded

Iris of her and her boyfriend when they were younger. They weren't really old, just not as young as this couple, which looked to be about in their early twenties. The magazines in the waiting area were good ones. She thumbed through a home décor magazine and read short articles on how to decorate a room for less. She loved contemporary looking furniture. Clutter wasn't acceptable in the apartment. They were both neat. She was neater than him and sometimes he appreciated her for it.

The medical assistant called the last name of another woman seated in the waiting area with her. In thirty minutes it would be her turn. She thought of what she would share with her therapist. She needed to dump her thoughts and do it all at once. There was so much to share.

She hoped Dr. Morgan would offer some sound advice to help her make the kind of serious decisions she needed to make in order to propel her life forward. She wanted a sense of peace. Her phone vibrated in her purse. It was Kevin. He was such a handsome guy. He was also tall and intelligent. He was a natural at baking and his measurements were exact. He knew how to fix cake problems such as sinking, falling icing, and over baked cake. His grandmother taught him how to bake. He had dark curly hair that stopped just below his earlobes. He kept his beard low and his eyebrows bushy. There must have been something wrong at the bakery. She stepped into the hallway outside the office space to take his call.

"Hello boss."

"Hi, is everything alright?"

"Yes, this is not an emergency of any kind, but I have a minor issue to discuss with you."

"Ok."

"A customer brought in a coupon for ten dollars off any special occasion cake. It's from the mailer we sent out locally."

"I remember this mailer. What's your concern?"

"Well, the coupon expired yesterday, but the birthday cake she ordered was due today for pick up. The customer is wondering if we can give her the discounted price despite the expiration date." There was a brief silence between them. She could tell by his tone that he really wanted to give the customer the discount. "Is it for one of our regular customers?"

"Yes, she's ordered several cakes from our bakery in the past two months."

"Sure, that's fine. Give her the discount." He was pleased with her response, especially since he had assured the customer that he didn't see why he couldn't make this exception for her. Kevin was an excellent team leader. He led others in the bakery without being overbearing and too bossy. "Thanks for clearing this with me first. See you a bit later today."

"Ok, I'll tell the others. Have a good one." She ended the call and returned to her seat in the waiting room. Her entrance alerted the medical assistant. A large, kind-faced woman looked over the counter and said, "Dr. Morgan will be with you in a moment." She nodded and picked up an entertainment magazine before sitting down.

Iris skimmed articles about celebrities and imagined herself in dresses she admired on famous actresses. One actress was wearing a black lacy evening gown. It was floor length and fitted. It also shimmered. The dress was a designer one that the stylist chose for the actress to wear at a movie premiere. She heard her name called. Finally, it was time to vent. She inhaled deep and quickly let it out. While walking, she could feel her heart race. Dr. Morgan's office was at the end of the hallway. There was a window at the end of it. The sun was almost blinding. She felt it warm the left side of her body as the medical assistant opened the door, entered, and then allowed her to do the same. Upon entering, she placed her purse on the stand adjacent to the door. Dr. Morgan was seated at her desk, writing. "Good morning, have a seat where you feel most comfortable. I'm just signing a few papers for my assistant and then we can begin." She smiled at her therapist and sat in a large chair. The fabric on it was light and plush. There was a matching one across from the chair Iris was seated in. Dr. Morgan sat in it, greeted her with a smile, and placed her yellow note pad on her lap. Both were silent. This was the process.

After a few visits to therapy she learned how their sessions would go. Dr. Morgan waited for the client to talk about whatever was on her mind. When she felt the need to interject with a comment or question she would, otherwise she listened and took notes. She didn't know where to start or what to share first. Her therapist already knew that she was unhappy in her relationship with Steve. During the last session Iris shared that she wanted to leave her boyfriend. This is what she told the doctor: "I thought I was truly ready to end it with him and walk away from the life we've shared over the past five years. I can't do it." Dr. Morgan noticed her client struggling to share. "Why do you feel that you can't leave him?"

"I still love him. I realized this the other night at dinner. I cried so much that evening because I was trying to avoid telling him how I really felt inside. He was the perfect guy when we had dinner together and the next day he was the same perfect guy." The doctor jotted some notes. "I thought he was pretending to be kind to me so that I wouldn't leave. I wondered if his interest in me, my job at the bakery, and saving our relationship was sincere. He hadn't been concerned about any of these things for over a year. We were strangers who came and went to the apartment we shared, but aside from this, there was nothing more between us. Every day there was pain in my heart. If he felt anything for me at all, I certainly couldn't tell. We had a date a few days ago. We went to the museum, which is something we have only done one other time and that was years ago. It was wonderful being around him. He was funny and loving. It was as if everything had changed back to the time when our love was real to us and obvious to others. A time when we were unashamed to feel so strongly about each other."

"What made the date memorable for you?"

"Well, we had to wait in an extremely long line before entering the museum. He didn't get angry. The fact that it didn't bother him that we had to wait, surprised me. I kept thinking the real Steve, who was an impatient jerk, would come out at any moment. But I was wrong. The date was perfect and there's nothing I would've changed about it."

"It sounds like he's putting forth more effort to meeting your needs. Isn't this what you want?"

"I do. But now that I have his attention, I'm torn about accepting it. I fear there's some sort of scheme he's concocted to lure me to stay and work on our relationship. My heart feels compassion and love."

"Have you discussed these emotions with your boyfriend?" "Somewhat. He keeps telling me that he wants to work things out. He even suggested we go to counseling. And this is another thing that surprises me about him. Years ago when I suggested it, he thought it was a ridiculous idea. He was absolutely against doing exactly what I'm doing right now with you. He's unaware that I've been seeing you."

"What's preventing you from telling him the truth?"

"I won't tell him. I can't. I'm afraid of him judging me. He would think that I'm a psycho. I also think that he'd be upset with me for keeping this secret from him. "If he ever found out, I'd lose."

"A good relationship isn't a competition. You've said that lately your boyfriend has been nicer to you, why do you think he would act differently if you tell him that you're seeking help for your feelings?"

"I don't feel comfortable taking the risk. There's another issue that I have with him." Iris paused for a deep breathe. "Yesterday, while I was in the guest bathroom, I found a receipt in the trash can. It was from a restaurant that we've never been to. The time on the receipt was stamped at a time he said he'd be working late. Now I don't trust him. I think he's been cheating on me."

"How do you know that it wasn't a client that he met for dinner to discuss business?"

"I don't know. I've thought about asking him, but he'll think I'm accusing him of something that he'll probably deny and then hold it against me. I just had an awkward feeling in my stomach when I opened the crumpled receipt. I questioned whether or not there was anything for me to get upset about. I wondered was this jealousy I was feeling. Why do I even care if he's been seeing another woman? A week ago I was adamant about leaving him and now I'm wavering on that decision." Iris let tears fall. Dr. Morgan grabbed a few tissues off the desk and handed them to her client. "The last year has been terribly stressful for me. We've ignored each other so much that I feel partially responsible for the reason he may have chosen to seek affection elsewhere. There's always someone out there that will fulfill a man's needs, especially if you're not willing to. I wasn't. I was numb. I didn't care that he was the most attractive man I've been with in my entire life. I didn't care that he was financially stable. I also didn't care that he hung out with his buddies from work several times a week."

"How did you manage to avoid interacting with your boyfriend?" "I immersed myself in work at the bakery. All I cared about was work. I allowed it to consume me."

"You are only making matters worse for yourself by avoiding them." Iris knew that her therapist was right. "I had a minor panic attack at the museum. One minute I was fine, staring at artwork and the next minute I was pouring sweat, trying hard not to freak out. I got away from Steve as fast as I could and I tried to remain calm enough so that he wouldn't notice anything wrong with me." Dr. Morgan stopped taking notes as her client spoke. "Since our previous session how often would you say you've had a panic attack?"

"It was the only one I've had since that time. I think what triggered the attack was that I began considering working things out with him instead of just ending it. The thought of staying with him frightened me. I don't feel that he's a horrible man, although I've tried to convince myself of it because we've been like strangers this past year. He's shown me the side of him that I love. I want it despite everything that has transpired between us."

The session with Dr. Morgan left Iris feeling a little better than she did when she first entered the office. She released some of the anxiety over keeping secrets from her boyfriend and felt inspired to talk to him. She wasn't ready to tell him about being in therapy. She grabbed her things from the office and as she walked to her car her stomach growled. It was still early enough for her to grab breakfast. She decided to go to the park and eat the lunch she'd made. Her head began to throb while she walked to the car. She wondered if it was the start of another panic attack. When she arrived at the park, she sat in her car for over an hour. She let the seat back and stretched her legs forward. She closed her eyes and tried to relax. She didn't have another attack. She felt fatigued. She would spend the day alone. She sent Kevin, the team leader at the bakery, a text message saying that she was taking time off today to rest and that she would be in tomorrow. He sent a simple "ok" as a reply. This put her mind at ease.

The park was quiet. She found a bench near a tree and ate the turkey sandwich. It was a sunny fall day. The jacket to her pants suit was enough to keep her warm in gentle winds. She watched a woman push a baby

stroller toward the playground area. The woman
had a little boy who was toddler age. He
hobbled to the slide and tried to lift his
short legs high enough to climb onto the
bottom of the slide. He fell and began crying
because he couldn't do it. The mother ran to
her son's aid and picked him up, holding him
in her arms. The woman rubbed the toddler's
back and rocked him side to side, shushing him
until he calmed down. When he stopped crying,
the mother climbed the slide with him in her
arms. She would attempt to slide down with
him. It was a risky move.

Iris drank a beverage and watched the two
of them. At the top of the slide, the mother
swung her child across the front of her body.
He was excited and glad to be in his mother's
arms. She held onto the side of the slide
until she felt she had a good grip on her son.
The mother let go and down they went. At the
bottom the mother's feet landed in the sand
and she let out a yell for joy and the son
clapped his small hands together. He was
smiling wide. It made Iris smile too. She
wanted a child. The birds chirped. She enjoyed
sitting alone on the park bench. She thought
about Tina. Her phone vibrated. It was Steve.
She ignored the call. He would assume she was
busy at the bakery and she would call him back
later. He didn't leave a message.

At work he thought of Rene and the things
she'd said to him in conversation. It was best
that he distanced himself from her. One day he
and Rene could possibly be friends. Ending all
communication with her was best for now.

BEST FRIENDS

Rene was devastated by the way things ended with Steve. She needed to express her feelings to someone she could trust. Her best friend was that someone. She could tell her anything without fear of being judged. It didn't matter to Rene that her best friend might psychoanalyze her problems. She could use a little therapy. They met for brunch at Orange Peel, a new restaurant downtown. In the past, they had spoken about giving it a try. Today was the perfect day for it. Outside the weather was warm. It felt like a spring day, although it was fall. Rene drove to the restaurant feeling uplifted about her brunch date. Her best friend often had an extremely busy work schedule. She was already booked with patients eager to share their woes for the next three months. She paid for parking and the valet took her keys. She entered the crowded restaurant and was immediately greeted by a young hostess. She was wearing casual clothing. The décor was contemporary with an urban edge. The floors were dark hardwood. The tables were white with high-back chairs with soft ivory cushions and metal legs. She saw her best friend seated alone at a small table for two. Their eyes met and they both smiled.

Dr. Lacy Morgan stood up and then embraced her. "Hi, how are you?" she said, smiling. "I'm well. It's so good to see you again." They sat down and Rene dropped her car keys inside her purse. "What a nice bag, where did you find it?" Lacy said. "Isn't it lovely? I found it on sale at Milan's. It's a new boutique that opened about a month ago on Michigan Avenue. We must make time to shop there together," Rene said. They had been friends since college. Rene majored in accounting and Lacy majored in psychology. They met one night when the café at the university served nachos and ice cream treats. They were both insomniacs who often stayed up late to study for exams. That night they talked about their studies and professors at the ice cream table filled with a variety of delightful toppings for vanilla, chocolate, and strawberry soft serve ice cream. Rene had a little of each flavor topped with candy sprinkles in a plastic bowl.

Lacy was more reserved with just vanilla ice cream and granola as a topping. They felt connected to each other and became friends right away. Lacy helped Rene through all of her failed relationships even after they'd graduated from college. Lacy had little time to date anyone. Grad school and a part-time job consumed most of her time. If she did go out with a man she had an interest in, it wouldn't last because she rarely had time to spend with him. The guy usually became bored with dating her and soon she was single again. She didn't mind being alone. Lacy believed that when the time was right she would meet that special guy who would understand and respect her work. She was passionate about being a therapist. She loved to help others work through their personal problems in life. She knew that her best friend would have much to tell her about the things going on in her life.

They looked over the menu. The breakfast items all included ingredients that seemed delectable. Rene ordered scrambled eggs and a Belgium waffle. Lacy chose buckwheat pancakes and an egg white omelet. Both requested a glass of freshly squeezed orange juice, which they sipped as they conversed. "How's the therapy practice going? Have you met any zany clients that you would rather not listen to?" Lacy giggled and said, "You know that I can't discuss client information with you; however, business has been consistent and although I haven't met anyone I'd rather give the boot to, I've been feeling sort of drained lately. The long hours have left me little time to sleep. I find myself looking forward to the weekends until I have an emergency call from the hospital, telling me that someone needs my assistance. It's quite challenging at times."

"I bet it is. Honestly, I don't understand how you can listen to so many different scenarios from so many different people and not be a little crazy from it all," Rene said. They both laughed at her comment and sipped more orange juice. There weren't many people in the restaurant. They arrived in time to miss the rush of business patrons who normally pack the place. Lacy liked the open feel of the layout and the quietness. She noticed the wait staff was efficient and friendly. Their waiter was a middle-aged, bald man who had well-manicured nails. He also had huge calves that were visible through Levis. Lacy noticed them as he walked away after serving them breakfast. The food was hot and smelled delicious. Rene generously poured on the maple syrup and smeared the whipped butter topping into her waffle. Lacy watched her as she tore into her plate of food like a starving sailor away at sea. They ate in silence for a brief moment.

Lacy was eager to hear what her best friend had been up to. She was curious about whom Rene had been dating. She wondered what the guy was like and if he was a good looking man with a great job. She hoped he was single and not married or in a relationship with someone else. "So how's life been for you since we last spoke?" Rene chewed and swallowed a waffle bite then let out a short sigh. "Well, as usual work has been busy. All day long I crunch numbers, balancing the budgets for CEOs that could care less about my name. I just landed two new major accounts this month and I've had to go over their books several times to double check figures a senior accountant claims he thoroughly reviews daily. The work isn't difficult. It's mundane at times." Lacy nodded her head in acknowledgement of Rene's thoughts about her job. She took mental notes. She had been a senior accountant for six years and she was well compensated for her expertise with money. "Is there any way you can minimize the workload you have and maybe devote more time to a hobby you find enjoyable?" There it was. Lacy couldn't resist being a therapist even with her closest friend. She was a natural, it was in her blood to try and fix people's lives. She always offered Rene a suggestion for making life better. She did the same for her clients. They appreciated her for this consideration. It's the reason why she did well in her practice. Clients couldn't get enough of her guru advice.

In college, Lacy considered writing an advice book. She never did it, although Rene thought she should and encouraged her to do it. "You know you really should write that book." They both laughed at this.
"You should also meet a nice guy sometime in the near future." "You know how short I am on time. I haven't met a guy who can deal with that."

"Well, you have to make time for it. What
about signing up for one of those online
dating sites? It seems like it's really common
nowadays for singles who want to meet someone
nice."

"The thought of it makes me highly
uncomfortable. You have to expose a ton of
personal information to strangers. You have to
filter out the weirdoes who sign up for those
online dating sites. You even have to pay a
monthly fee, which just seems over the top."

"True, but what are successful, single women
like us going to do to find Mr. Right?"

"Wait. Are you single again? I thought you met
a nice guy the last time we talked.

"Well, I thought so too until he dumped me a
few days ago. He did it over the phone."

"Oh, that's awful. I'm sorry things didn't
work out for you."

"Me too. I was drawn to him and I believed he
felt the same way toward me. But then again I
should've known things between us were never
going to amount to anything that really
mattered."

"Why do you feel this way?"

"You know it's always the same case for me
with men. I don't want to bore you with the
details."

Lacy touched her hand and said, "You never
have to worry about this. We're friends and
I'm here for you."

Lacy had no idea Rene was about to reveal that
the man she'd been dating was her client's
boyfriend. Rene knew that her best friend was
the most sincere person she'd ever met in
life. She told her everything about Steve. The
nice guy who was no longer hers and who had
never really been hers from the start of their
relationship. "I met him in the deli at work

on the main level of our building. I went in for a turkey sandwich to take back to my cubicle. Standing there looking at the refrigerated items for something to eat was the most handsome guy, wearing a designer suit, I'd ever seen. He was hot. I tried to ignore him. The scent of his cologne made me feel high. I walked past him over to the section where the sandwiches were and he said hello."

"That was all it took, huh?" They giggled.

"You're absolutely right. You remember how lonely I was after my break up with married man Pete."

"Oh, that took you a long time to get over." Lacy thought Pete was the ultimate scoundrel. Not only was he a cheater, but he was also an abuser. He almost wrecked Rene's self-esteem. He made her feel inadequate from the moment he knew she had fallen in love with him. Lacy helped her realize that she deserved better than Pete and she was so happy when she was finally done with him. "I looked into this handsome guy's golden brown eyes and I was instantly hooked on him. He was well built with glowing, copper skin, and he was so charming. I really tried hard convincing myself to only return the greeting and then keep it moving."

"Sure you did." Lacy shakes her head from side to side.

"He was quite persistent in getting to know me. After we introduced ourselves and chatted about the best, cheap sandwiches in the deli, I wanted to get to know him better. He paid for our food and then gave me his business card. That's how I learned that he worked in the same building as I did, except he was on another floor. I also noticed that we were in the same line of work."

"So you were intrigued with this guy because of his looks and your shared career interests."

"Exactly, he was attractive and a numbers man. What more could someone like me ask for? I didn't use the number on his business card right away. I wasn't certain if I wanted to get involved with anyone, especially after my ordeal with Pete."

"How did the two of you connect?"

"He sent a note card with my daily office mail. He wrote: Lunch on me at the deli today at one o'clock. It made me blush." "You've always been into arrogant guys."

"True. And I liked that he showed some initiative. I'm not easy to find in the company and he only had my first name to go on. I still don't know exactly how he found out which floor I worked on. I mean there has to be over a dozen women named Rene in the building. I was completely taken by this man and I wanted a free lunch if nothing else was to come of our next meeting."

"Now that part I understand."

"I arrived a few minutes before our scheduled time to meet and I waited around in the lobby area for him. At one o'clock sharp he was walking toward me after leaving the elevator. I couldn't believe this was happening. The whole situation made me feel like a kid." Rene shifted in her seat to cross her legs.

"What were you wearing?"

"I had on a flowing, teal dress with a thin black belt around my waist. I wore simple accessories in silver. I had on black patent leather heels too. I felt so pretty that day. We greeted and then he gave me a gentle kiss on the cheek. He gave me a compliment and that made me blush again."

"You're so easy."

"Right. I knew then that he was attracted to me. He had on a navy suit with paper thin, light blue stripes on it. It was another designer suit and not the kind from an outlet store. Those eyes, girl, his flawless smile made my heart flutter." Lacy leaned back in her chair, turned slightly so that she could cross one leg over the other. "This all sounds perfect. What made him end it?" Rene sighed and said, "I assumed he was single, but he wasn't. He lives with his girlfriend and they've been together for several years."

"Are you kidding me?"

"No, and I wish I could tell you otherwise because I know what you're thinking." Lacy almost slipped into therapist mode when Rene told her that she had been dating another claimed man. This trend had to stop and Rene was the only one who could do this. She had to end the cycle of dating men who weren't single. If she ever wanted to be in a healthy relationship with a man that believed in commitment and boundaries, she had to stop settling for less. Lacy avoided sharing her true thoughts. "I'm not judging you at all. I know this is difficult for you. You shouldn't think that I wouldn't listen with an open mind." Rene withheld tears when Lacy held her hand again. She felt sincerity and trust from her best friend. Her support and warmth right now was needed more than ever before.

The waiter came over to clear the table. Lacy called her secretary and requested that she reschedule all afternoon appointments to the next day. Luckily, she had an opening slot the next morning otherwise she would have to make it up to her clients with a discount or additional session time without charge. Her clients were regulars so they didn't mind the shift in appointment time and date. As long as they had an appointment with Dr. Morgan they were content. Relieved to have a good, long girl talk, Rene slipped off her heels. She ordered a bottle of white wine for them. As they sipped wine Lacy wanted to know more about the handsome accountant. "We never did anything more than engage in a few kisses. We almost had sex. We went out for lunch and dinner quite often and we talked every day. He never seemed uneasy about being caught when we were out together. It made me forget that he had someone. He was attentive to me. I became oblivious to the fact that he'd leave me and go home to his girlfriend."

"Wait, did it ever cross your mind when you were out late in the evenings with him to question, what is his girlfriend thinking about his whereabouts?"
"No, not at all, and looking back now I know that if I were in her shoes I'd wonder what he was up to several times a week. We both worked hard at our jobs and most of our conversations centered on work related issues. He even helped me figure out a problem I was having balancing a budget for a client. I trusted him with every part of my life. I know this may sound strange to you, especially since we hadn't known each other that long." "How long did you date this accountant?"
"It lasted about seven or eight months. It felt like it was a much longer time."
"How did you find out that he had a girlfriend?"
"He told me on the second date when we met at the deli again. It was really our first

official date. He was calm and honest. I mean what guy comes right out and tells you he's unavailable and then pays for lunch? I found him fascinating and his honesty made me think I had a chance with him. We claimed our budding relationship was a friendship, although he made it clear that he wouldn't be pleased if I decided to see someone other than him." Lacy slowly shook her head as she reached for her glass of wine. She didn't approve of Rene being gullible. "His feelings were definitely one sided and a bit selfish on his part. Why do you think you continued getting to know him despite awareness that he had a live-in girlfriend with whom he was in a committed relationship?" Rene took a moment to think about the question. It was a typical longwinded one that only a therapist could ask.

She gulped the wine in her glass. "Well, Doc the more time I spent with him the more connected I felt with him and it was probably foolish to think this way, but I believed he would leave her." Lacy glared at her and said, "Really? This is the same feeling you had with Pete."

"You're right, except that he wasn't like Pete. He said his girlfriend wanted to end things and that they had been living under the same roof with tension between them." Her best friend was silent while she continued to speak. It was as if Lacy had slipped into a trance. She felt herself go foggy mentally while Rene's words continued to come out of her mouth, but she only saw the movement of her lips. The sound was muffled. Rene didn't notice that Lacy was day dreaming as she spoke about her feelings for Steve, the handsome accountant she met in a deli, who had just dumped her. Lacy thought of Iris, a client she'd seen on a regular basis for years. She thought of their most recent session. She had been in a relationship with an accountant and they were about to break up. *Rene has been dating my client's boyfriend*. Lacy hadn't thought of this until now. Both women had been involved with Steve. This was not a good thing for her. She couldn't mention to Rene that she personally knew Steve's girlfriend. It would be a breech in client confidentiality, which was a highly regarded rule for her. She also couldn't tell Iris that she was right about her suspicion of her boyfriend seeing another woman. A dilemma that she didn't want to be a part of. She was renowned and respected as a therapist in the community, plighted to help others make better life decisions so that they could avoid mistakes like the one Rene was still describing.

Lacy snapped out of tunnel vision. Rene's voice came back clearly as cloudiness lifted. She had been babbling the entire time. "I just fell so hard for this guy and now he's gone and there's no chance of us being together again." Lacy concealed her discovery of whom Rene was speaking of. "How do you know for certain things are over between you and this accountant?"

"He said that he wanted to work things out in his relationship and that he loved his girlfriend. As upset as I am over this, I know in my heart that being done with Steve is the best thing for me."

"I agree with you and as I always say, -- Rene interrupted, "You deserve better." Lacy paid for the lunch and they hugged goodbye. Rene walked to her car now feeling less stressed. She appreciated the opportunity to have someone listen to her relationship blues. She drove back to the office. Dr. Morgan walked to her car, a Mercedes, hopeful that Rene and Steve's involvement was finished. She listened to messages on her voice mail. Shocked over the news Rene shared with her, she decided to talk to someone who helped her with matters of the heart. She searched through the contacts on her cell phone and landed on her mentor, Dr. Friedman. Much time had passed since they'd talked about anything.

In college she was an intern for Friedman, who was the head of the psychology department. She admired and respected him and she also could trust him to give her sound advice she desperately sought. Friedman, a mature man in his sixties, was an expert therapist. She recalled how calm he was with his clients. He let them sit anywhere in his office. This is the reason why she did the same thing with hers. Friedman taught Morgan how to set up her office in an inviting manner. To place the furniture in spaces where clients might still enjoy natural sunlight or a feeling of privacy while talking about their personal matters. Since she had the rest of the afternoon off, she called him to see if he could spare some time to meet with her. She needed his advice on this matter with Rene. She feared she couldn't keep the news a secret. She might find herself out of practice for violating patient confidentiality. Torn, she wanted to be a good friend. If Rene ever found out that she didn't disclose what she knew, she might lose her best friend of over twenty years. Emotionally confused about the decision she had to make, she almost cried. She vowed to be ethical as a therapist, but there was the aspect of being honest by just telling her friend the truth. It tugged at her heart.

Surprisingly, Friedman answered his phone. Sometimes he would do this if he was free and didn't have a client. This was the case for him today. He told her that he had an opening in his daily schedule. He was more than happy to see her, although it was on such short notice. She hurried to his office. Lacy was now the patient being greeted and told to *have a seat anywhere in the room you feel comfortable*. She sat in the chair directly in front of his desk. She rubbed her hands, while looking down at them. They felt cold and clammy. This was unexpected. Friedman stared at her. His glasses rested just below the bridge of his large nose. He had a hunch that she would share something major.

He opened the center drawer of his desk and placed the yellow notepad inside. He was silent and patient as he waited for her to speak. He wanted her to do it freely without any pressure she might feel from probing questions. "I've just learned that my best friend was dating my client's boyfriend. They were together for several months before he finally called it off. I'm torn Friedman. I want to tell my client that her boyfriend has been cheating on her, to confirm her suspicions, and to advise her that she should stick with her decision to leave him. I know it's wrong. This would ruin my professional status as a therapist who's supposed to adhere to patient confidentiality regardless of the information I receive."

She shifted in her seat, paused for a deep breath in. "It's not like this is a crime. People cheat on their partners all the time and some of them manage to stay together in happiness despite their indiscretions. I'm uncertain why I can't shake this feeling to tell. I know plenty about my clients' personal lives, which I've always kept secret. Now it baffles me that I'm taking this matter so personal." Friedman kept his eyes on her while she spoke. He made a mental note of her expressions and body language. The way she fidgeted with her hands, periodically darting her eyes from them to look at him or an object in his office. "My best friend shouldn't be involved with this guy and I'm really glad that he was mature enough to end it. But I know she hasn't gotten over the thought of what could've been. I feel lost on this matter. I know what's right, but I believe that I should act on it in some way." Lacy rose from the seat and quietly paced the room, with folded arms. She stood by the curtains near a window and waited for her mentor to speak.

In a low, raspy voice Dr. Friedman said, "Clearly, you've attempted to work through feelings on this issue. What's troubling you most?" She turned to face him. "It's the first time I've had to deal with being close to the matter. I know that I won't say anything to my client or my best friend about it. But I feel like I should. Ignoring the feeling that I should tell bothers me." Friedman nodded.

"My credentials mean everything to me. People respect me and depend on an unbiased approach to help them untangle any drama they've created in life."

"Everything you've shared is valid, yet impractical. You're human first and this is not a flaw. No one is perfect. You've expressed common feelings that we all experience when we genuinely care about others. Do what you feel is best." His advice eased her worries. In silence she sat on the floor near the window in his office for another hour. There was nothing more to be said between them. His presence gave her comfort. Reassurance that somehow everything would work out fine.

THE TRUTH

Iris drove home after sitting alone in the park until sunset. She garnered the strength to confront Steve about the receipt she'd found in the guest bathroom. Her heart insisted he was cheating on her. *Hearts never lie.* When she thought of the receipt, it made her cringe with anxiety. She wondered whom he had fallen for and if he would continue to see the other woman. *Was she pretty?* She hadn't dealt with the reasons why he may have stepped outside their relationship to begin with. The reasons did matter to her. That would have to wait.

She took a longer route home. Light rain began to fall. She let tiny water droplets fill the entire windshield before she pressed the wipers to clear them away. She repeated this process until she pulled into her apartment complex. The drive home was peaceful. The only noise she heard was from rainfall. She missed several calls from Steve. Each time her phone vibrated she ignored it. When she thought of returning his call from earlier, she imagined him setting up a lunch or dinner date with another woman. Anger welled up inside her. If she couldn't shake this emotion she would be defensive and this would cause an argument. She was tired of arguing over things she felt would never change. How they managed to stay together through years of mostly silence, tension, and distance between them confused her.

She put the key in the door lock and looked up at the ceiling, closing her eyes before turning it to unlock the door. They rarely used the deadbolt lock above the doorknob. He was seated at the dining room table, still in his suit, when she slowly entered through the door. He looked up from the table. His face was so handsome even with a stern look on it.

"Hey."

"*Hey?* Is that all you have to say to me?"

"For now, yes."

"I've been calling you all day with no answer. Why didn't you return my calls?" The tone in his voice was a mixture of concern, confusion, and irritation. The vein on the side of his forehead was showing. He had a slight frown on his face as he spoke. She tried to remain calm and in control of her emotions. If things escalated into an argument it might trigger a panic attack. "I had a busy day." It was a lie. He knew it. "I called the bakery and after the third time and several badgering questions from me, Kevin finally told me you weren't coming in. What in the hell were you doing all day? Where were you?" She was exposed. She had to answer his questions otherwise he'd continue to interrogate her. Her palms began to sweat. A sign of a trigger for a panic attack. "I had lunch with a friend and then I went to the park." Her response frightened him. He knew that she liked sitting in the park. Sometimes she went just to watch people. She told him once that watching people gave her ideas for cakes. He suspected her visit to the park was more about him than icing for cakes. It meant that she wanted to end the relationship. He felt nauseous. It was hard to accept that the woman he wanted to eventually marry, have a kid or two with, and spends the rest of his days analyzing numbers, eating cake and turning grey with didn't share his sentiment. He loved her so much that it hurt. "Next time could you please just let me know this? I was worried about you that's all." He waited for her to say something. She sat in a chair at the table and rubbed her eyes. He relaxed his shoulders and said, "I need a shower."

When he left the room, she kicked off her shoes and thought of how she'd approach discussing the receipt. She pulled it out from a pocket inside her purse. She had smoothed out the crumples as best as she could. *Was he as kind to her as he was with me at the museum?* He rubbed a fluffy white towel back and forth on his naturally wavy hair, cut low, and then wiped the mirror. He wondered what to say to her. He wished for something profound to say to Iris. To make her forget about leaving him. He believed he could make her the happiest woman alive, instead he fouled up the longest relationship he had with any woman. He dressed in a t-shirt and shorts. She was standing near the kitchen counter when he came out the bedroom. He noticed her staring at a small piece of paper. She felt his arms around her waist, the warmth of his embrace, and the moisture on his chin against her neck. His affection aroused her. She closed her eyes, enjoyed his kiss. He lowered his shorts and tried to unzip her pants, own her right there in the kitchen.

She jerked away from him the moment her eyes opened and saw the receipt. "What's wrong?" Holding up the receipt, she turned to face him. "This is what's wrong." He stared at her with a confused look on his face. "What the hell are you talking about?" He snatched it out of her hand and glanced at it. "Why are you upset over an old receipt? Did I forget an important date or something?" She glared at him with her arms folded across her chest. "That's exactly what I was thinking when I looked at that receipt last night." He held it up again and shook his head a little. "Perhaps you should take a closer look at," she said. He tried to smooth out the wrinkles in the receipt. His eyes narrowed as he recognized the name of the restaurant. When he looked into her eyes, he saw that she was searching his for answers. He felt an ache in the back of his throat. If he told her the truth it would be the end of their relationship for good. He couldn't take that kind of risk. This would ruin the trust she had all along for him. He had never given her a reason to believe that he would cheat on her. He never thought he would cheat. There was no way he was going to expose his relationship with Rene. He felt there wasn't any need to do this. He'd already dumped her and had no plans of ever seeing her again. She watched him and waited for his response. *Why is he taking so long to say something?*

He realized that Iris was suspicious, but didn't know who he'd taken to Jimmy's Crab Palace. It was an escape from admission of guilt. Lying was his only option. He hoped it would minimize the argument brimming between them in the kitchen. "This is nothing. It's old. I went there with buddies from work about a month ago. I didn't think it was worth mentioning. Things were different between us then. We were barely speaking to each other. I didn't even think you cared about what I did during this time. I didn't even think you would even care to know who I hung out with either. Why are you making such a big deal over this receipt?" Her facial expression softened and she unfolded her arms. His plan was working. "I thought you might have gone to dinner with another woman who wasn't a potential client."

"What gave you such a ridiculous idea like that?" He laid the receipt on the counter and leaned in close, kissing her on the cheek, and then said "I don't want any other woman but you. Don't you know that by now?" She wanted to believe him. Something deep inside her gut wouldn't let her. She felt he was covering up the truth. She accepted his affection and dropped the issue, although she didn't believe the excuse he gave her. Steve was relieved. Once again he saw how she truly felt about him. If she didn't love him, she wouldn't care to know the truth about the crumpled receipt. He was careless to throw it in the trash can in their apartment. His arrogance was on a pedestal higher than the mantel in the living room. For now he'd succeeded at keeping the truth hidden, but eventually he would have to tell her. "Would you like something to eat? We could get Mexican food this time." She nodded in agreement, pulled away from his arms, and went to the bedroom. She sat on the edge of the bed, waiting for food to arrive. He despised the tension hovering like a storm cloud inside the apartment.

BEST FRIENDS FOREVER

Rene was alone in her bedroom when the phone rang. It was Lacy. She invited her out for lunch and shopping. They enjoyed shopping together, especially when there was a huge sale on designer items. Lacy wanted to be certain that Rene had given up on the dream of being with her client's boyfriend. She had no intention of telling Rene what she knew. This would mean the end of her therapy practice. They decided to shop before having lunch at the Potato Hut. Outside a boutique they admired a white, floor length evening gown on display. It was form-fitting and hung perfectly on the mannequin. Lacy believed Rene would look stunning in the gown and Rene thought the same about her best friend. They debated on the price of the gown and to settle it they went inside to speak with the clerk. A tall, thin man immediately greeted them upon entering the boutique. He wore a navy blue blazer and European style pants in black. The store was tiny. Clothing and accessories were strategically placed on the racks, the walls, and in the main aisle. Customers could see everything in the store from any angle. "Good afternoon, ladies, can I help you find something special today?" Lacy turned toward the mannequin in the window display. "It's a beautiful gown, isn't it? I can pull one in your size and place it in a dressing room for you."

Rene smiled and told the salesclerk Lacy's dress size. She was caught off guard, but appreciated Rene's spontaneity. She had been this way since college. If she hadn't spoken up, Lacy would've never stood inside the dressing room, staring at her reflection in a beautiful evening gown. She felt like the most beautiful woman in the boutique as she pulled back the curtain to the dressing room and stepped out so that Rene and the salesclerk could see her. Rene's eyes widened as she stared at her. "You look absolutely beautiful in it!" The dress fit her body perfectly. Rene encouraged her to purchase it, but she refused. She had nowhere special to go in such a pretty dress.

Lacy told Rene she should try one on in her size and she agreed. The salesclerk was certain he had a sale from one of them. The gown was priced at fifteen hundred dollars. Rene looked impeccable in the gown. "It's a shame that I have no one to get dressed up for." The salesclerk was disappointed when he realized neither of the two women would purchase the evening gown. Lacy bought a pair of dangling crystal earrings and Rene bought a monogramed coin purse. The clerk was pleasant, but wished he'd made a larger sale from them. He wrapped and packed the items in small, gold paper bags with matching ribbon on one handle. The women shopped for an hour longer and then drove Rene's car to have lunch at the Potato Hut. It was a popular bar and grill type of restaurant, known for its exclusive potato menu, and crowded with patrons. "There's a thirty minute wait for a table unless you'd like to sit in the bar area," the hostess said. They chose to wait.

When a booth became available, they ordered loaded potato wedges and drinks. She was careful to approach a conversation with Rene that was unlike one of a therapist and patient. "How's everything been with you since our last outing?" Lacy was terrible at this, she asked a question that was exactly like one she'd ask a client seeking advice. Rene didn't quite pick up on it right away. She thought her best friend was genuinely concerned about her well-being. She set a glass of wine on the table and said, "I've been busy with work so I haven't had time for much else. I did a couple of workouts at the gym. That was rough. I need to get back into going at least five days a week." "Well, you've managed to be physical at least, which is better than doing nothing; besides, you look great." A short waitress with hairy arms brought the appetizers. They tore into them. The appetizers were so delicious and filling they skipped the main course and ordered dessert. "Have you spoken to that guy you were dating?" Rene chewed a small bite of triple layer devil's food cake that was on her fork and wrinkled her brow. "I haven't heard from him. Sometimes I still think of him, actually every day, but I'm completely over him. I can't be with someone who's unavailable to me. You even said so when we last spoke. I know that in the past I've made the same mistake more than once." "How can you be certain that you're over this guy?"

"I'm done. Another lesson learned."

"What if he calls you, how will you handle it?" This was exactly like Lacy to keep probing with questions about a matter. She was searching for answers. Something felt strangely odd to Rene about the line of questioning. They were all related to the same issue. Rene didn't really feel the need to discuss the breakup again with her or anyone. "You seem extremely interested in the guy I dated. I feel like there's something you're not telling me. Do you know him?" Rene was keen. Her job required her to look beyond the numerical facts listed on a client's books to expose if someone had been embezzling from the company. Her skill in this area is what made her notice that Lacy was concealing the reason why she wanted to know more about her interaction with Steve.

Lacy avoided making eye contact with her. She feared she might break down and tell her the truth. Rene watched her closely, waiting for her to speak. Lacy tried to keep her composure. Her hand shook a little as she lifted a piece of cheesecake to bite. She kept her gaze on the plate while she chewed. "I just wanted to know if you were handling this better than your last situation. I'm sorry if I made you feel any sort of discomfort. We're friends and I'm trying to be a good one to you. I know you're deeply hurt by it. It's completely normal to find it difficult to let go." Rene stopped eating her cake. She glared at Lacy and said, "You've said a lot, but you didn't answer my question." Lacy reached for her glass of wine, turned it up, and gulped it down. *She's my best friend, my only friend. I can't tell her the truth.* "I can't share what I know with you, but as your friend I am telling you that you've done the right thing by not pursuing any kind of relationship with him. Lacy sat back in her chair and thought about how Rene might react to what she had just said to her. Lacy believed she was clever, not too transparent with her secret; however, she didn't deny that she knew something about Steve.

The waitress threw her head back slightly to move the long bang covering her left eye as she walked toward their table. She grabbed the plates and laid the check face down on the table. Lacy pulled out her credit card at the same time so that the waitress could take it.

It wasn't often they had a chance to shop and have lunch together. Rene thought it was a setup. She felt a twitch above the eye. "I can't believe you're doing this!" Rene said and pounded her fist on the table, rocking it. Startled by her reaction, Lacy felt the eyes of others staring at them. "What do you mean? And what's wrong with you?" Rene leaned forward, tightening her mouth as she spoke. "You know exactly what I mean. I've known you long enough to know when you're lying. You planned this entire day all for the purpose of finding out more about Steve. You aren't being honest with me." Rene slipped on her heels and stood up. Lacy rose too. "Rene, please don't be upset with me. I care about you. And you're right, but I can't say anything about it." "So you do know him? I knew it! This is so like you to pry for information and then clam up when you're caught. Coward." Rene smacks her and it causes Lacy to stumble a little backward. Stunned, holding her cheek while others watch them. It took a moment to register that her best friend had hit her. It was a hard hit. Guilt kept her from retaliating. "This is foul. I don't know if I can ever forget this moment with you. And now that I know you're withholding vital information from me, how can I ever trust you?"

"Are your serious? You're being unreasonable. You're not trying to understand things from my perspective. I have a reputation to uphold and if anyone was to find out that I violated patient confidentiality, I would lose my practice."

"Bullshit. You weren't so concerned about your idiotic oath when you told me you knew him." Rene grabbed her purse and shopping bags. She stormed out through the revolving doors at the entrance. The corner edge of a shopping bag was lodged in the door and ripped as she pushed her way out. Lacy considered chasing after her to try and convince her that the apology was sincere. She rubbed her face. Weighted by the reality that she'd lost her best friend, she couldn't move a muscle. It was best to allow Rene time to deal with her emotions.

MORE THERAPY

Iris arrived to work early dressed in casual attire. Today she had to be the first one at the bakery. She rarely wore jeans to work. Stretchy light denim against her skin made her feel awkward. She cared more about the receipt than her outfit. Steve had lied to her. Instinct led her to believe that he wasn't honest with her, although he gave an excuse. An extended one, on the spot like good liars do. *He's never taken me to Jimmy's Crab Palace.* She filled trays with miniature cakes and placed them inside glass cases in the storefront area. On a whim she scheduled an emergency appointment with Dr. Morgan to discuss more of the things troubling her. When she phoned the office, she was on hold for ten minutes. This was strange, an uncommon wait for regular patients. There it was again, good old suspicion settling in. If the man she loved could look her straight in the eyes and lie to her, anyone could do the same. She had no reason to doubt Morgan's character, but waiting made her uneasy. The receptionist said, "I've put you down for tomorrow morning." She felt a slight relief from this news. It was another chance to vent. She greeted a few staff members who had just arrived for their shift and retreated to her office for the rest of the day. After closing the bakery she avoided Steve at home, claiming she had a headache, and went to bed.

The next day she entered Morgan's office and the waiting room was empty. *Odd, there's always at least one other person waiting to see her.* She tried not to dwell on it instead she focused on her emotions. Hopeful therapy would help her discover solace, what's been missing for several years from life with

Steve. She thought for certain he would admit that he'd been involved with another woman. She could handle the truth. Deal with it on her terms. Try to work through this matter with him or leave him, which was the original plan. Doubt fueled her panic attacks. She closed her eyes to quiet voices in her head while waiting to speak with Morgan.

"Iris, I can see you now," Morgan said and then smiled. She stood in the open doorway. They greeted each other and Iris followed her therapist down the corridor to the office. There was a cool draft in the hallway. She never questioned why Morgan came to get her from the waiting area. Something was off about the visit. In the office she lied on the sofa. It felt right to do. When she began therapy, she would lie on the sofa and ramble about whatever was on her mind for the entire session. Morgan would sit quietly and listen to her while taking notes on the things she shared. She wanted to cry, but couldn't do it. "How are you feeling today?" "I want my boyfriend's neck chopped by guillotine. Morgan shifted in her chair, remained silent while her client spoke. "He's a damn liar and I wish I had proof of it so that he would have no choice, except to confess. I confronted him last night about the receipt I found inside the trash can in our guest bathroom. He didn't recognize it at first, but when he looked at it closely he realized what it was. His facial expression showed he'd been caught doing something wrong."

"How did you react to his behavior?" Iris turned her head to look directly at Morgan. "I waited for him to tell me the truth. I didn't say anything to him and I could tell that my silence made him a little uncomfortable. He said that he went to Jimmy's Crab Palace with his buddies from work. It was a good excuse. But he was lying and I knew it. I couldn't argue with him. All I have to rely on is my gut instinct and that isn't really enough. I let the matter go and we ate Chinese food while watching television. We didn't talk about it anymore or anything else for the rest of the evening."

"What could you have done to make that night better?"

"I should've called him a liar. In bed there was no affection between us and that didn't bother me at all. The only thing on my mind was getting the truth about that damn receipt. It kept me awake all evening." Morgan stopped writing on her notepad and said, "You know in your heart when something is off kilter. You've been in a relationship with your boyfriend long enough to notice when changes occur within patterns of behavior. It seems that he hasn't been entirely truthful with you. You have every right to question his actions, especially since you've recently tried to reconcile your differences." Morgan heard herself giving Iris the kind of advice that was meant for a close friend. She was crossing a very risky line with her client. If Iris assumed that Morgan was providing her with general advice to help her manage problems this would be fine. If she suspected her therapist had information about Steve, she would not be able to weasel out of revealing the truth to her client. Iris sat upright on the sofa. "Do you think my boyfriend's a liar?" Morgan dropped the pen in her hand and leaned back in her chair. She wanted to simply say *yes* and then accept the consequences of her actions. It was unethical to do. "What you're feeling is valid. Go with it. No one can alter your feelings on anything you believe to be true." *A yes or no would have been better.* Iris inhaled deeply, slowly releasing the air from her lungs, lowered her head on the sofa, and crossed one foot over the other. After a few moments of silence she said, "I kissed a woman who works for me. I liked it."

A WEB

Rene stared at her cell phone as if she was waiting for an important call. *He dumped me. Just let it go*. The incident with Lacy was a spinning top in her soul. Emotions that she never knew existed stirred within her. For the first time since her involvement with Steve, Rene was jealous of Iris. It was unfair that his girlfriend enjoyed a life with the man she wanted by her side. To both women he had been deceitful and selfish. Steve told her everything that transpired in his "bad" relationship. She put her chin in one hand, wiped tears with the other one before they streamed her face. She felt betrayed. *How could I be so foolish, falling for his lies*? She allowed it. She had no one else to blame except herself. She wanted revenge and she knew exactly how to achieve it.

She called Steve, something she hadn't done in over three weeks. The call went straight to voice mail. Instead of hanging up and redialing to annoy him, she left a message: *"Hello, this is Rene in case you've forgotten. Your girlfriend knows about me. If you would like to know how then call me."* She hoped this would make him call her back. Steve's face and name appeared on screen almost immediately after she ended the call. He couldn't believe what he'd heard her say. *How could Iris know the truth*? Fear outweighed his confusion. More than anything Steve had to keep his dealings with Rene a secret. He didn't want to speak with her again. He suspected a setup. But he had to be clear about the message she'd left him. He wasn't in the mood for niceties. He only wanted to get to the reason why she'd left the message. On the first ring she answered his call.

"What's going on?"

"It's good to hear your voice. How are you?"

"Listen, I'm not interested in a long discussion. Care to explain your message?"

"Fine. Apparently, your girlfriend has been seeing a psychiatrist to help her deal with your failing relationship." There was a brief silence.

"What the hell are you talking about? That's completely ridiculous and you don't know anything about my girlfriend. I can't believe that you would stoop so low and make an accusation like this. I don't have time for-" Rene interrupted before he could continue his rant. She couldn't tolerate his arrogance.

"You're wrong! I know that your girlfriend is in therapy. In fact my best friend is her therapist."

He felt as if someone had knocked the wind out of him. In a calmer voice he said, "Are you serious?"

"Quite. I found out yesterday while we were having lunch. She didn't mention her name, but she said enough to lead me to believe that your girlfriend is one of her clients. I just thought you should know."

The news was hard to accept. *Could it really be true? Why is Iris in therapy without me?* He closed his eyes, while rubbing his forehead. He recalled her jealousy over the receipt she'd found and wondered if there was any connection to it. Then he thought about the messenger on the other end of the call. He was suspicious of Rene's motive. *Why did she share this with me?* He had dumped her and by doing so hurt her. He shook his head a little. "Wait a minute. Why in the hell do you care who she's seeing?" He didn't let her respond. "If there's any truth to what you've said it's still none of your business." She succeeded at making him feel flustered. She wanted to shatter his hope of reconciliation with Iris. "I don't care if you don't believe me. Ask your girlfriend about Dr. Morgan and find out for yourself if what I'm saying is true." Rene hung up.

Steve put the phone in his pocket and let out a long sigh. He walked back inside the building with clenched fists. As he waited for the elevator he decided to stop on Rene's floor and confront her. He had to see the expression on her face to confirm if she was being genuine about her claim. He had to be certain of whether or not she'd fabricated the entire matter. If she was right, it would be disastrous for him. He'd have to explain to Iris how he even found out that she was in therapy. He'd be forced to tell the truth about his dealings with Rene. He shook his head as if it would clear his mind from racing with what-ifs. The elevator doors opened to the seventh floor. Rene was standing in the lobby area. She looked beautiful in a form fitting coral dress and high heels. She had great legs. He wasn't surprised to see her there. She knew he would come. They had spent quite a bit of time getting to know each other's personality. She knew that he was the type of guy who demanded clarity. He would probe her with questions until he got the kind of answers that satisfied him. He knew that she, although a jealous type, wasn't a liar.

Rene's heart raced as he walked toward her. She was attracted to his stride, strong jawline. She imagined wrapping her arms around his neck and pressing her lips against his. A stern look on his face was clue that he wasn't in the mood for any sort of romance. Steve had both hands in his pockets. When he got close enough to her, he felt drawn to her. He wanted to lift that dress, put his hands between her thighs. He'd not had sex in a while. She unlaced her fingers, positioned her arms down by her sides and received his kiss on the cheek. She felt mushy inside and almost forgot about her plan of revenge against him. She was in love with him. It blocked her will to stay angry at him. His scent mixed with cologne made her feel light-headed like when they'd first met. He was handsome in a tailored black suit. "Can we go somewhere private and talk?" She agreed. They rode the elevator to the main floor. They walked outside, around to the side of the building and sat in the covered eating area for employees. "Are you absolutely certain that what you've told me about my girlfriend is true?"

"Well, my best friend didn't flat-out tell me. But yes, it's the truth."

"This is crazy. I don't know why she's in therapy."

"You can't know everything about a person. Everyone has secrets."

"I guess so." Rene grabbed his hand and gently rubbed it. She wanted him to embrace the idea of being with her and forget about his girlfriend so that they could be happy together. Looking at her flawless skin, full lips made him weak. He knew he should've withdrawn his hand from hers. He enjoyed her touch. The way the tips of her manicured nails gently scratched his skin intensified his desire for her. While he waited for her to say something else to him, he felt tempted to slip back into his old ways. Desire attacked his sense of logic. Iris was furthest from his mind. For the first time, sitting across the table from Rene, he regretted not taking things further with her when he had the chance the night they passionately kissed in her apartment.

"You said this doctor is your best friend, but why would she share any form of personal information about one of her clients with you, knowing what's at stake?"

"I'm sure she's aware of the risks. Listen, she didn't tell me directly, but I was able to figure it out from the way she was questioning me about my relationship with you. I told her we had parted ways. It was just a normal conversation between close friends. I trust her with any and everything in my life and it's been this way for us since we were in college."

He believed the sincerity in Rene's eyes. She was telling the truth and as difficult as it was for him to accept, he knew that he had to speak to Iris about this when he arrived home. "I don't know what to say except thank you. I'm so blown away by it. I need time to think about this. I feel like I don't know who she really is now." Rene could tell that he was conflicted and deeply in love with his girlfriend. It made her insanely jealous. She jerked her hand from his, stood up, gave her dress a tug so that the hemline fell right at the knee, saying, "Well, good luck with that," and then walked back into the building. After a few minutes of watching her hips sway he followed her, keeping his distance. Inside his office he leaned back in a swivel, black leather chair with a pen in his hand that he was clicking repeatedly as he thought about how he would approach this issue with Iris when he saw her. He could smell Rene's sweet fragrance on his tie. He felt a pang of regret. *Why am I even entertaining the thought of rekindling a relationship with her?* She wasn't the one for him, but now for some reason he doubted whether or not Iris was the one.

MEET THE DOC

The next day at work Steve slumped in his chair, staring at the computer screen. The numbers on the account log blurred. He rubbed his eyes to bring them back into focus. He lost the nerve to confront Iris about seeking therapy. He was curious about the reason she chose therapy and surprised that she'd been so clever at secrecy. An idea came to him. He searched the Internet for Dr. Morgan. There were several doctors in the area with that name, but only one who was a woman. He called the office and made an appointment to see her. On the spot he pretended to be someone else. He gave the receptionist a false name and claimed that he was having major anxiety and job related stress. It wasn't totally a false claim. He'd experienced a tremendous amount of anxiety after hearing Rene's news. He enjoyed the work he did as an accountant. The pressure to meet deadlines and put money back into the hands of corporate heads gave him a rush. Dr. Morgan was booked with appointments until the following month. Steve couldn't wait that long to see her. He embellished the truth further by claiming that his symptoms of anxiety were extremely high and that he considered committing suicide.

The receptionist immediately gave the phone to Morgan's head nurse. The nurse spoke to him about his suicidal thoughts and then miraculously he was able to secure an appointment with the doctor for the following morning. He hung up pleased with the outcome despite having to break out crying over things that were completely fabricated. That night he went home and continued to appear as if there was nothing on his mind, although he was anxious to ask his girlfriend about Dr.

Morgan. He couldn't risk ruining the chance to speak to her therapist. He had doubts. Iris was the perfect woman: beautiful, intelligent, and successful. He was curious to know the reason why she needed counseling. The only way to unveil the truth was to show up at Morgan's office and confront her about the issue. He wondered whether or not he should mention Rene's name. If she found out that he'd gone to visit her best friend she'd be furious with him. It didn't matter. Blinded by arrogance he disregarded the fact that Rene had an ulterior motive. He believed she truly cared about him. He had no idea that she wanted him to be hurt, to feel some agony when he learned of his girlfriend's secret.

That night they had a brief conversation about work and stuff they saw on television. They even shared a good laugh over a favorite commercial. Everything appeared to be normal between them. In bed, he kissed her on the shoulder and turned his back to her. For a moment Iris was concerned that he made no attempt for intimacy, but she was relieved to fall asleep next to him without worry of having to deny affection beyond the kiss. No advances convinced her that he'd been cheating. In time the truth would surface. The next morning Steve dressed in jeans and a white button-up shirt. He didn't appear as a man suffering from anxiety and high stress. In the kitchen he smiled at Iris. She was making coffee.

"Is it casual day at work?"

"It's a nice day out. I feel like I need the change. Do you think anyone will notice that I'm not wearing a suit?"

"Looks like you've already made your choice." They drank coffee and sat in silence. She noted every move he made. He checked emails from work and sent one to his secretary to give notice that he'd be in the office by noon. He checked his watch for the time. Kept smiling at her each time he looked up from his phone. *He's acting strange*. They left the apartment and took the elevator down to ground level. Their cars were parked next to each other. Steve kissed her on the cheek and said "Have a good day." She wanted to ask about his sudden change in mood, instead she said "You too," and got in her car. Both ignitions roared in the parking lot. She pulled off and he followed her out to the main street near the building. They drove in opposite directions. She took local streets to the bakery. He got on the highway and drove beyond the speed limit to Dr. Morgan's office. She looked in the rearview mirror for his car. *Why did he take a different route to work*? She saw a vehicle that was exactly like the make and model of his car, but realized when the driver switched lanes and drove past her that it wasn't him. *Where did he go*?

STEVE AND MORGAN

When Steve arrived at Dr. Morgan's office, there was only one other patient waiting to see her. He tapped on the armrest of the chair he sat in. He tried to appear patient and calm while he waited. He thought of the things he might say to the doctor. He imagined himself inside a dull office space that was dimly lit. He would tell her a fake story about his stressful job and how it made him want to end his life and then he'd ask her was she treating his girlfriend. He had several questions for the doctor. She had to answer them otherwise he planned to expose her, ruin her career.

The nurse called his name and he followed her to Morgan's office. Her office was more inviting than he'd imagined it would be and Morgan was an attractive woman. "Thanks for seeing me on such a short notice." His palms felt clammy. He thought of backing out of his plan until she said, "No worries. Have a seat." He sat in the chair in front of her desk. She always requested that new clients fill out a brief questionnaire to gain insight on how to best meet their needs. They were silent while he darkened in the circles for questions related to smoking, anxiety, suicide, and substance abuse. After filling out the form Morgan told him how she liked to conduct therapy sessions and then gave him a tour of the office. He followed her around the office and listened attentively while she spoke.
"How long have you been a psychiatrist?"
"For over ten years."
"I bet you see plenty of patients with crazy stories to tell." He was shadowing every move she made in the room and the closeness made

her feel uneasy. Morgan sat in a chair near the sofa, interlaced her fingers and said "I help people resolve their issues. What would you like to discuss today?" She hoped that this question would encourage him to be open about the reason he needed an emergency appointment. He shoved both hands in his pockets and cleared his throat before reclining on the sofa. "I have a hectic workload. Sometimes I have a hard time trying to balance accounts. I lose focus and feel pressured by the demand to keep up with daily deadlines. If the numbers are off with a client's books, I could be fired on the spot. My boss holds me responsible if anything goes wrong with the client's money."

"What exactly do you do for a living?"

"I'm an accountant." She stopped writing on the notepad and looked at him. A knot formed in her chest, making her breathing shallow. She realized she hadn't noticed how handsome he was. He didn't appear to be suicidal or stressed. He was too calm. *This is not happening right now. Is he my client's boyfriend?* Morgan appeared to be calm. She didn't want to expose her suspicion. He noticed her staring at him and felt this was the perfect moment to ask her about Iris. "I think you know who I am, that is, if you don't already have an idea. She didn't flinch or say anything. She kept her gaze on him. He was right, but she was hesitant to confirm it. "Listen, I don't want to play games here. I have reason to believe that my girlfriend has been coming to see you on a regular basis." She got up, placed the pen and notepad on her desk, and stood by it with her arms folded. *The nerve of this guy.* She thought of threatening to call the police.

142

"I'm unable to disclose any information to you about my patients."

"Are you sure about that?"

Morgan could tell that he was not the type to back down from a challenge. She couldn't allow herself to be so easily rattled by his arrogance. She wanted to yell and curse at him for wasting her time. She sat and leaned back in her chair. It was a pleated, burgundy leather chair. Steve sat upright on the edge of the sofa. "I'm not trying to cause you any trouble or anything like that. I just want to know if Iris is a patient of yours. I would also like to know why you've been seeing her." Morgan saw desperation in his eyes, a love-stricken man who would do anything to save his failing relationship. *He's a liar. Who cares?* Telling him what he wanted to know wasn't worth the risk of losing everything she'd worked hard for in life.

"Let's say that your girlfriend is one of my clients, how does this impact your feelings toward her?"

"It wouldn't make me feel any different toward her. I love her with all my heart and I want her to believe that I do. Obviously she's chosen to keep this a secret from me because she feels that I may judge her for it. Honestly, I don't mind her seeing you. But I don't like that she's kept this hidden from me. I wonder what else she hasn't told me. Can you at least tell me if I'm on the right track?"

"I can't."

"I know that I've gone about this all wrong. I'm sorry. I just want to fix whatever is troubling her. We've spent the last year of our relationship mostly in silence and this can't continue if we're going to improve our relationship." Morgan knew that the longer she listened to him the harder it would be to withhold the truth. "I can't disclose any information to you. As a professional this would be unethical. I suggest that you speak to your girlfriend. Find a way to work things out with her." Steve let out a sigh and rubbed his forehead. "I could really use your help." His voice trembled. "All I want is to know the truth."

"I understand. Has your girlfriend ever expressed an interest in therapy for any reason at all?"

"She's mentioned it, begged me to go when we were having problems. I refused to go to therapy. I thought it would be a total waste of time." Morgan sat in her chair and let him continue. Curiosity made her want to hear his side.

"My girlfriend was withdrawn from our relationship. We became strangers who barely spoke to each other. I felt lonely. I knew it was wrong, but I began seeing someone else." She was aware of whom he was speaking of. She ripped the page from the notepad she'd jotted notes on. "The woman I was seeing is a close friend of yours, right?"

"We're not discussing my personal life. Patient confidentiality is a serious matter. I've already told you I won't reveal anything to you about my patients." She stood up and tossed the paper ball in a small trash can near her desk. "It's time for you to leave."

"Your job as a therapist is to help others get through personal dilemmas in life so that they can live a happier one. Why are you refusing to help me?"

"You've come here under a false pretense, expecting to bully me into providing you with

144

information." He rose from the sofa and walked toward her while saying, "I don't want to upset you. Please just tell me whether or not you're friends with Rene. She's not a patient of yours so you wouldn't be violating any laws by at least telling me that much." He made a good point, although she was irritated by his persistence. "I will only tell this if you agree to leave my office and never try to contact me again." He shook his head a little and said ok. "I've known her for many years. She's my best friend."

They were silent for a moment. She stood near the chair closest to where Steve was standing with a worried look on his face. He knew that she wouldn't budge with any further information. He wanted to know if Iris had any clue that he'd cheated on her. "Now please leave." He was about to leave her office, but he couldn't do it. "I'm sorry that I've brought this problem to you. I truly didn't know what else to do. My girlfriend means everything to me. She's my universe. I don't think I can survive without her. My life would be over." His dark eyes glistened at the rim. He was on the verge of crying in front of a woman he'd just met. He couldn't believe this was happening to him. He would never consider showing vulnerability if things hadn't gone terribly wrong in his relationship. He could no longer withhold the tears that streamed along his cheeks and strong jaw line. Morgan's mood softened. She felt empathy as he wiped his face with the back of his hand, embarrassed over tears. She wished for the kind of love he felt for Iris. She offered him a tissue and he used it to wipe the corner of his eyes. "You have turmoil that must be dealt with. Have a seat." He continued to talk to her for over an hour. He shared his deepest feelings for Iris and he talked about how things had changed between them. He wanted to reverse time to when they were madly in love. A time when they saw forever in each other's eyes. He hadn't spoken to anyone, not even his closest buddies about the real reason why the relationship began to unravel.

"I never meant to hurt Rene. I care about her. She's loving and kind. She was there for me when I needed comforting." He realized as he shared his innermost thoughts and secrets that he needed help. "If you had continued to hold these feelings inside they would've damaged your chances of learning how to deal with them. To improve your relationship with your girlfriend, you must work on the things that are troubling you. To avoid them only makes matters worse." He nodded in agreement while she spoke. Morgan forgot that she'd asked him to leave. "I want to move beyond the trouble we've had in the past. I never wanted to ignore her and it went on far too long. We seemed to slip away from each other. I made excuses for not spending time with her. I stopped being loving and affectionate to her for no apparent reason at all. She didn't do anything to provoke the insensitive mistreatment she received from me. One day I awoke and felt so angry. About what, I don't know. I couldn't shake the feeling all day. When I arrived to work, everything bothered me. Routinely I had a tremendous amount of work to do. I craved it. I felt overwhelmed this day and the people I worked with got on my nerves. I thought everyone was an idiot."

Morgan sat with her chin resting on her knuckles, listening to him pour out his heart. He cried so much in front of her until his eyelids became swollen and sore from wiping tears. Morgan yanked a few more tissues from the box on her desk and handed them to him. "My cubicle was near a guy that smacked and popped his gum. Normally, I could ignore it, but on this day the guy really ticked me off. He smacked the gum while he chewed it and then he repeatedly popped it. I imagined getting up from my office chair, walking over to where his was, and punching him in the face. The guy was twice my size, but I didn't care. I left work early that day. I claimed that I was feeling sick. When I arrived home, I didn't speak to Iris as I entered our apartment. She was sitting on the sofa watching television. I walked right past her, into the bedroom, and closed the door." He put his head in his hands. "I have so many regrets. I realize all the mistakes I've made. I'd give anything to make things absolutely perfect between us. She deserves nothing less than a man who would give her everything that her heart desires." Morgan leaned forward in her seat and said, "We all go through difficult times in life. You're doing the right thing by dealing with these emotions. There's no need to feel embarrassed. Be as transparent with your girlfriend as you've been here and seek counseling for couples. You might learn that you both share the same sentiment. She wouldn't have stayed with you through one of the most difficult times of your relationship if she didn't harbor the same love you share for her." Her voice calmed his nerves. The advice gave him hope. He was no longer concerned with the reason why Iris was seeing her. He knew that it was beneficial to have her as a therapist. Now all he cared about was making things right. He left the office

feeling ready to tell his girlfriend the
truth. He opened the sunroof of his car and
took the long way home.

TIME OUT

Luckily, Dr. Morgan didn't have any other appointments booked for the rest of the day. Drained by her experience with her client's boyfriend, she plopped on the sofa and lied there with her eyes closed. *What if I had confessed everything I knew about the women in his life*? She hadn't and this made her feel triumphant as a therapist who believed in maintaining an ethical code of conduct and professionalism. Then she felt like a hypocrite. In her last session with Iris she eluded to the fact that she was right to assume that Steve had cheated on her. She wanted her to end the relationship. He was deceitful. He didn't deserve to have either woman. It hurt to know that Rene had betrayed their friendship. *How could she do this to me*? Lacy sat up to remove her blazer, kicked off her high heels, and again reclined on the sofa. She clasps one hand around the other and rests it on her forehead. *What did Rene think she'd gain by telling him the truth about his girlfriend*? She thought of the last time they were together and felt the sting from being slapped hard across the face. She had to speak with Rene. She wanted to know why she would jeopardize her career.

Lacy shook her head back and forth repeatedly, trying to avoid crying. Too late. Tears splashed across her face like waves coming to shore. She punched the back of the sofa and began wailing. Her face contorted. She was frustrated that things had spiraled out of control. She never wanted to become entangled in it. *Pull it together. This is not your fault.* She worried the others outside her office could hear her. She would have to explain the noise. *Are therapists supposed to cry*? She let tears stream until she fell into a deep sleep. The tapping on her door was unheard as Lacy slept sound in her office. The assistant entered the office after she didn't get a response. She peeked in and saw her boss lying on the sofa. The office was dimly lit. She had closed the main office area and was about to leave. Lacy hadn't come out the office after Steve left. "Is everything ok?"

"Yes, I'm fine. I was a little tired."

"I'm heading out. Is there anything you need me to do before I leave?"

"No thanks. Have a good evening." She sat upright and watched her assistant close the door.

FALLOUT

Almost a week had passed and still no word from her. Lacy left several messages on Rene's voicemail. Each one was the same: *We need to talk so call me back as soon as you get this message*. It was crude of her to tell Steve about their friendship. This is how he found her. She understood the reason why Rene was angry with her. If there was a way that she could've told her the truth without risking her status as a therapist she would've done it. To betray the trust they shared as friends was wrong. *Whatever her motive was for telling him about me is irrelevant*. Anger coursed through her body. With pursed lips she stomped toward her desk. Now she was fuming. She'd been there for Rene throughout all her trials with worthless men. She would never do anything to hurt her or their friendship.

She grabbed her phone and pressed Rene's number. She had it on speaker. It rang several times before it went to voicemail. She took deep breaths to try and calm her racing heart. While she waited for the outgoing message to end, Lacy thought of leaving her cordial message like the previous ones, but anger took over. At the beep she said, "You stupid Bitch! How could you do this to me after all I've done for you?" and hung up. The release of anger was a good one. It empowered her. She called her again. This time when the beep sounded she said, "You're such a coward and a fool. Don't bother returning my call. I never want to speak to you again!" She powered off her phone and tossed it on the desk. She thought of going home. Then she remembered the bottle of white wine in the mini refrigerator. It was a gift from a client in gratitude for help dealing with loss. Lacy poured wine in a tall glass and paced the office floor. She drank the entire bottle and passed out.

Rene listened to the message Lacy left for her and was nervous about returning the call. She knew her best friend would be angry with her for what she had done. She was shocked to hear her curse and yell. It was unlike her. She knew that there was no way that she could explain her way out of this matter. She knew that Steve would take some sort of action once she told him the news. She regretted telling him. She worried that he might have harmed Lacy. It was too late. The damage was done. She rammed the cell phone against her head. She was certain their friendship was over.

Lacy awoke past midnight. The alcohol made her feel lightheaded. It slowed her movements. Furniture in the office looked slanted. She was in no condition to drive so she called for a cab. The cab driver was a woman. She had a thick Russian accent and smelled like Goji berries. Her hair was bright red and wispy thin. Lacy scooted to the middle of the backseat. She was drunk. "Where are you going?" She gave the driver her address. Her eyelids felt weighted. She rocked in the backseat of the cab as if she was on a boat. She almost fell asleep until the driver alerted her that they were near her place. She gave the woman a large tip and staggered up the stairs to open the main door. As the elevator moved up each floor she floated with it. By the time she had unlocked the door to her place and undressed, she felt extremely drowsy. She sunk deep into her bed and slept.

The next morning, Lacy heard a muffled chiming sound coming from underneath the covers. She was groggy from the wine. It took a few seconds for the room to come into focus and for her to figure out that she was in her bedroom. The sound grew louder as she lifted the cover and saw what was making the noise. It was her cell phone. She reached for it near the foot of her bed and looked at the screen. It showed a picture that was taken last year when she and Rene were on vacation in Hawaii. They were smiling in bikinis on the beach. Lacy wore a sheer sarong over her bikini bottom. Rene was comfortable showing a lot of skin. She quickly sobered up and immediately felt angry again. She stared at the phone trying to decide whether or not to answer it. On the fifth ring she answered the call.

"Why did you tell him about me?"

"I didn't mean to."

"You're lying."

"What happened?"

"Your guy came to my office posing as someone else. How could you do this to me?"

"I never meant for you to be hurt in any way by this. I know it was wrong. There's no excuse for what I've done. I'm sorry." Lacy cried. She couldn't believe how easily her heart and attitude softened as soon as Rene apologized."

"I tried to prevent something like this from happening, which is why I refused to tell you anything about him. I knew it would only make things worse. And then you hit me. Why? I didn't deserve that!" She could hear Rene crying on the other end of the call. They cried together for a short time and then Lacy said, "The worst part of this ridiculous fiasco is that now that I've met him I understand how you could fall for this guy. He's not a horrible person like your last boyfriend. Peter was scum. He didn't deserve you. This other guy doesn't either because he's a cheater. But I don't think you're wrong to feel upset over things not working out with him." Lacy got out of bed and grabbed tissue from the bathroom. Guilt made Rene feel worthless, horrible inside. "Are you in love with him?"

"Yes and as much as I would like to ignore my feelings and walk away from this, I can't. Lacy blew her nose and wiped it clean. "Did he say anything to you about us?"

Lacy let out a sigh and said, "You always fall for the wrong guy." It troubled her to know that her best friend continued to make the same mistake with men. Neither of them had anymore tears. "You've betrayed me in a manner that most people in my profession can't recover from. It was completely irrational and stupid of you to do. You should've talked this over with me first before you made this decision." Lacy's tone was scolding and turning a bit cold as she spoke. Rene despised being chastised like a child. She wasn't in the mood for a lecture. The longer she listened to her the more resentment she felt toward her. She thought of the incident at the restaurant and it pissed her off.

"It's over. I can't take back what's happened and I don't care anymore. You don't give a damn about my feelings! When you realized that Steve was your client's boyfriend, you didn't even consider telling me the truth. How can you call yourself my best friend?"

"You're selfish and you've always been this way. I care about your feelings, and you know it. Doctors have an ethical code of conduct to uphold regarding patients. For once why can't you understand my opinion? It was you, not me, who created this mess! And you expect me to

trash all I've invested in building my practice to appease your selfish needs."
"Whatever. You act like you're a saint who never thinks twice about crossing the ethical boundary you're preaching about now. When you implied that you knew something about Steve, but refused to tell me, you crossed the line."
"You're unreasonable."
"I'm just stating the facts. You're clever. I didn't suspect anything from your questions about him. But you kept prodding me for answers to the same questions phrased differently as if I was one of your clients."
"What the hell was I supposed to say to you? Hey, by the way you know that guy you were dating? Well, he's my client's boyfriend."
"Exactly. At least it would've been the truth. I would've done that for you."

A swarm of memories hit Lacy. She thought of the happy moments they shared as close friends, Iris' panic attacks, and Steve's visit. She never wanted to be part of this web of deceit, love, and sorrow. Lacy admired her honesty, although Rene was selfish. She would always be this way. More than anyone she valued her as a friend. "I wanted to tell you. I should've told you." Rene was silent on the other end of the call. She knew it was difficult for Lacy to admit it. Each woman held the phone and sat in silence. Neither one of them wanted to continue arguing. The only thing left for them to do was apologize to each other. Surprisingly, Rene said it first and then heard *I'm sorry too.*

EXPOSED

Steve slowly ascends a metal staircase leading to the upper level floors inside the building. He liked the industrial look of it most out of all the other features and amenities they were shown when viewing apartments. He recalled the time when things were perfect between them. They did everything together. Now they were falling apart. He was hesitant as he stood outside the apartment door. He took three short, quick breaths and turned the key in the lock. Iris was in the kitchen dressed in a plain t-shirt and pink boy shorts, waiting for him. She was beautiful. He laid his keys on the kitchen counter to avoid her gaze. She stared at him and waited for him to turn around. He didn't want to be angry with her, but she'd been lying to him and he wanted answers.

"How was your day?"

"It was fine, just another day on the job. We bake, deliver, and sell some of the best cakes here in town and people appreciate what we offer." He listened to her. He could listen to her all night if this was what she needed.

"How long have you been in therapy?" Her eyes widened and she let out a tiny gasp. Then she folded her arms across her chest. *Stay calm.* "What are you talking about?" He noticed that she ignored answering the question, but he couldn't let her off the hook so easily. He moved closer to her. She tried to move out of his way. He blocked her exit, moved toward her again, forcing her to walk backward into the kitchen counter. His palms were face down on the counter, a barricade she could only escape from by kneeing him in the groin. She appeared uncomfortable and a bit shaky. "You're avoiding my question, I don't like that. Why haven't you told me about therapy?" She felt warm. If she focused on her fears she'd have a panic attack in front of him. It was time to tell the truth; besides, somehow he already knew some of it.

She was also tired of concealing this secret from him. She thought of the last session with Dr. Morgan and how it gave her comfort to have someone listen to her concerns. Iris was prepared to tell him everything. "Can we talk in the living room?" His brow wrinkled some while he looked at her. Then he relaxed his shoulders, slid the palms of his hands off the countertop, and removed his arms from around her. He followed her into the living room. Her heart was thumping louder than a kick drum. For a moment she sat silently on the sofa uncertain how to begin. He was silent too, growing impatient with her. He shook his head back and forth, gesturing his frustration. This caused her to take an even longer time to speak. Steve wondered if she would say anything at all. "Why is it so hard to talk to me now?" This wasn't a good start. It made her feel defensive. "Until recently you haven't shown any interest in talking to me. I'm not certain that I'm ready to talk about therapy, although I knew that eventually I'd have to share this with you." "I understand." He laid a hand on top of hers and gently rubbed her fingers. She jerked them from his grip. "I began therapy a little over a year ago. I found a doctor that accepted my insurance and from the moment I met my therapist I knew that I'd receive the help I needed. Things between us were terrible. I mean we barely spoke to each other. This was the worst part of living here with you. Seeing you each day and only making eye contact in the morning before we left for work made me feel like a stranger to you."

"I never wanted you to feel that way."

"Please let me finish." He nodded and remained silent while she continued to speak. "I can't explain what happened to us. Suddenly we didn't get along. I didn't know you at all." She began to cry. "You changed. Everything changed. I felt blamed and I still don't know the reason for it." She wiped her face with a soggy tissue he'd given her when she began crying. Steve cared deeply for her. "I came home after my first therapy session with the courage to tell you about my experience. You were dressed and ready to go out with some of your buddies from work." He dropped his head in shame. "I asked could we talk for a minute and you ignored me. You said that you were in a hurry to leave, although the game was scheduled to show live on TV two hours later."

They were in the bedroom and it was summer. She wore a lovely pink floral sundress. He loved to see her in dresses. She looked soft and feminine. Iris was right about his demeanor toward her and he felt awful as he relived this memory with her now. He gently grasped hold of her hand and she clenched his fingers. The energy between them was warm, supportive. "I pleaded with you to stay a bit longer so that I could tell you about my therapy session. I hoped that if you knew that mine had been life altering then you'd want to go with me. I was trying to do whatever was necessary to save our relationship. The love in my heart was marred by anger when you left that night."

"Babe, I'm sorry."

"You're apology does nothing for me. The only thing you cared about was your job and friends. I never considered you were seeing someone else. But I know it's true, right?" She stared at him. He shook his head in disagreement. This wasn't the time to confirm her suspicions. It would ruin them. One day maybe he would tell her about Rene, but not this evening. "I never wanted things to be that way between us. It was an awkward time in life for me. You're not solely responsible for what happened. There's no excuse for my actions. I'm a selfish idiot. I just hope you can forgive me." His reaction surprised her. "Would you like some water?" She nodded for yes. He went to the kitchen and pulled down her favorite drinking glass. A star was etched in the center of the glass on both sides. He dropped a few ice cubes in it. With a puzzled look on his face he poured water into the glass. He had a gut feeling there was something else Iris kept from him. If it was ignored he might not have the nerve again to ask her about it. The water spilled some as he carried it to her. "Thank you." She was grateful for his kindness all he'd done to try to make up for the past.

She had no idea how he would react when she told him about the panic attacks. The moment she decided to tell him this, her heart quickened its pace. She wiped moisture across her forehead with the back of her hand and lifted her top away from her lower back. *This can't be happening right now* she thought. She feared it was a mistake to tell him about the panic attacks. *I can't do this*. She began to panic thinking about how not to panic. The reaction was starting to build. She worried how he would feel toward her once he knew the truth. Steve saw redness in her cheeks. There was no way out. "What's wrong?" She heard the

159

words come out his mouth, but the sound was muffled and it was as if he was speaking in slow motion. Her hands felt clammy. She had to work hard to breathe normally. Every muscle in her body stiffened. Panic was winning, although she fought hard to hide her emotions and physical reaction. She leaned on the arm of the sofa and wiped moisture from her brow to the bridge of her nose. She envisioned Dr. Morgan telling her to remain calm. She closed her eyes, inhaled deep, and slowly released it.

"I suffer from anxiety and it causes me to have severe panic attacks." When she said this, she turned her head slightly to face him. Wetness in her armpits felt cool against her skin. She was embarrassed, but relieved that she'd finally told him the reason for being in therapy. For a while Steve was speechless. Iris kept her gaze on her hands resting on her lap. He didn't know anything about panic attacks. He wanted to ease her discomfort. He folded his hand around hers, looked at her and said, "I feel like a jerk for not noticing you were suffering. I know this was hard for you to share with me. You don't have to worry. I'm here for you. I'm terribly sorry for ignoring you and us at a time you needed me." She couldn't believe that this guy, the one next to her being apologetic, was the same man who had ignored her countless times and chose his friends over her. "I'm feeling a little shaky."
"Would you like some more water?" She nodded to say yes. The back of her shirt felt moist and cold against her skin. Again she pulled it out and away from her back, fanning herself to dry the remaining perspiration. The panic attack she imagined she would experience when

she told her boyfriend about therapy, didn't happen. He set the glass of water on the end table next to the sofa and cradled her in his arms. She felt safe. This she could handle. "I wish you hadn't felt that your panic attacks had to be a huge secret between us. I don't like that you kept this from me. Actually, I'm a little frustrated that you went a whole year without telling me." She tensed up her shoulders. "How did you manage to keep all the doctor's visits hidden from me and your employees?" He sighed and waited for a response. She pulled away from his grip and frowned as she looked at him. "You're frustrated with me?" He'd said the wrong thing, although he didn't intend to be harsh, especially not now since she'd been open about her feelings.

When Iris rose from the sofa, this wasn't a good sign. He feared she was already offended by his attitude. A coil of anger spiraled inside her soul as she paced the carpet. She felt his blame, judgment. Steve had to be the one in control. In the past he made it clear to her that he was better than her at making decisions. One day it happened while she was buying steaks from a local vendor selling them inside the grocery store not far from their neighborhood. The meat was Grade A in quality and she wanted to cook him a delicious steak dinner. To get his opinion, she called him to discuss what she was considering, but he turned the conversation into a debate, which made her feel like an idiot for bothering him. She changed her mind about buying the steaks. They had spaghetti for dinner that night. She wasn't letting him do this to her again, not after all that she had been through over the past year. She had tolerated a significant amount of mental anguish. Dr. Morgan had helped her learn more about who she was as a woman suffering from depression and chronic panic attacks.

"This is so typical of you to try to make me feel like I've done something wrong. The fact that we weren't speaking to each other is why I didn't tell you about my therapy. I'm not the only one to blame for silence."

"I'm not blaming you. You're right. Come back and sit with me."

"I don't want to sit with you." Steve saw a rage in her eyes that was unlike any look she'd ever given him before. He wanted a way out before things escalated into an argument. He rose and tried to put his arms around her. "Take your damn hands off me. There were so many times I tried to convince you to work through our differences when I didn't even know exactly what they were. It was like you woke up one day and turned into a stranger. Someone other than the person I'd fallen in love with. I wanted to spend the rest of my life with you!"

"I know. I want the same thing. Calm down. I didn't mean to upset you."

"Whatever. You don't have any reason to say that you're frustrated with me. I don't deserve this shit from you, not now and not ever again." His eyes were wide and his mouth was partially open as he stared at Iris. Her tone shocked him. He couldn't think of any instance where she had been this angry with him. Her voice was loud as she ranted. He thought she might punch him if he'd forced an embrace.

"A moment ago everything was fine. Now you're attacking me. What's wrong with you? I

162

wasn't the one keeping a secret for over a year! I don't understand this panic attack stuff. What is it? Something happen to you in childhood? What the hell are you so afraid of?" He put his hand over his forehead and stopped questioning her. He was highly irritated with her and the entire matter. She folded her arms and shifted her weight from the leg outstretched to the other one. "How did you find out I was in therapy?" She was furious and perturbed with him for not answering her. He was sitting on the edge of the sofa with his hands interlaced, head down, and staring at the floor. She began to regret telling him everything. "I had to gather the courage to tell you about my condition and for you to be so insensitive about it is disgusting." She stormed off into the bedroom and began taking off her shorts. In shock, he followed her. They were having one of the worst arguments of their entire relationship. They hadn't fought like this ever in all the years they'd been together. What began as an open discussion about the reasons she was in therapy turned into a shouting match about matters totally separate from this one.

In pink, lacy bikini underwear, she quickly walked over to the vanity and pulled out a pair of cotton sweat pants. "Where are you going? We haven't even finished talking." "Who told you I was in therapy?" He sighed heavily as he stood in the doorway leading to their bedroom, watching her. He couldn't believe what he was seeing. It was comical to him, but if she knew that he carried this emotion too, she'd go ballistic over it. He folded his strong arms across his chest and crossed one bare foot over the other one as he leaned against the wall. He watched in silence

as she took out a pair of white ankle socks
from the second drawer and then walked quickly
to the closet to grab her running shoes. From
there she also grabbed a zip-up hoodie to
match her sweat pants. She glared at him with
slightly pursed lips. Then she shook her head
a little and avoided his gaze. "I'm done
here." She waited for him to move out of the
way. Steve was confident that he could
convince her to stay and talk things out. He
stood straight and then placed his hands on
her shoulders. "You don't have to leave. I
really wish you wouldn't run away from this
moment, although it's uncomfortable for both
of us. We can work this out if you give me a
chance to explain my point."
"Who told you I was in therapy?" Iris listened
as he spoke in a calm tone.
"I never meant to make you feel awkward in any
way whatsoever. I also really appreciate you
telling me everything. I just want to help
you. Please don't go." She was angry and
couldn't relent this time. She felt that he
wasn't being sincere. "Are you going to move
out of my way?" He turned sideways to let her
pass. He stood in the doorway to the bedroom
and watched her walk toward the kitchen. He
heard the sound of keys clanking as she slid
them off the countertop. Steve was astonished
that she was leaving. This was a new reaction
from her. One that he normally used when he
didn't care how it might affect her or their
relationship.

Iris had no clue where to go as she left
the apartment. She had to escape while she
could before she calmed down. She always
forgave him soon after an argument, although
they never resolved anything when this
happened. While she ran down the metal

staircase she decided that going to the bakery was the best spot to cool off alone. She wished she'd told him it was over between them. Steve slumped on the edge of the bed. He sulked about the argument. She didn't have to leave. He wanted to go after her and convince her that he never meant to hurt her feelings. But he also felt fine with her being gone. He thought she overreacted. He doubted whether or not the life they'd shared was worth fighting for anymore. After so many years of being together, he believed they were nearing the end. He thought of Rene and wanted to hear her voice.

CRUSH

It was sunny and warm outside. Iris drove with the windows open. Her hair lifted in the wind. She parked behind the bakery and entered through the back door. The aroma of lemon cake greeted her as she walked past the baking area. She turned on the light in her office and hung her jacket on the coat rack near the door. She plopped in her chair and laid her head against the back of it. She was no longer angry. There only an overwhelming sense of sorrow. She'd spent a year in therapy working through emotions and learning how to handle her condition. This wasn't supposed to be the outcome for someone who had exhausted all measures to make things right in her life. She heard the sound of the security alarm beep, alerting her of someone entering through the front door of the bakery. She didn't move from the chair. She knew the person entering was her team leader. Kevin was the only one besides her who had the alarm code. Permission was required if any baker wanted to work overtime. She needed their help, especially before the holiday season.

He turned off the alarm as soon as he heard the front door click close. He walked to the bakery floor and saw a dim light at the bottom of her door. He smiled when he realized she was in her office. It was more than a crush. He adored her and thought she was gorgeous the first time they met. He respected her as co-worker and eventually as the boss. He never shared his interest in dating her. Like Iris he had been a loyal employee at the bakery for over six years. They had worked together since the doors opened. Before Joan died in a car accident, he was promoted to team leader, which is similar to the position

166

as store manager. Everyone was devastated by the news of her death. On the day of Joan's funeral they shed tears, listening to Iris speak about a wonderful woman whom they had admired, respected, and learned a tremendous amount of things from since they began working in her establishment. They wanted to continue her legacy of providing the most spectacular cakes in the city.

Kevin walked toward the office door and heard her voice greeting him. "Hey, I didn't expect anyone to be here this late. How are you?" It was close to midnight. He'd planned to get an early start on cake orders for the next day. He also suffered from insomnia and couldn't fall asleep most nights without sleeping pills. He lived alone in a condo not far from the lakefront. "I'm surprised you're here. It's so late." She wasn't really surprised, Iris was aware that he'd worked late at the bakery on multiple occasions. Small talk was fine for now. Anything to take her mind off her troubles was welcomed. This was the first time she'd noticed that he was an attractive man. He was tall with golden brown skin and dark curly hair. He looked content in a plain, white t-shirt and light denim jeans paired with running shoes. They were worn out around the sole. He stood near her desk. She was slumped over it, resting her chin on her hand. He sensed something was bothering her. Iris looked like she'd been crying. He was hesitant to pry into her personal life and ask her what was wrong. He suspected that she wouldn't share anything with anyone unless she felt comfortable. He wanted to comfort her, rub her shoulders. She imagined running alongside Kevin in the park. The weather was hot and sunny. The grass was greener than usual and there weren't that many people on the trail. Fantasizing about a man who was standing right next to her desk was weird. She looked up at him and he was smiling at her. He had a perfect smile. It was warm and inviting.

"I suffer from extreme insomnia. I've had it for years." Without any prodding from her, Kevin openly shared something personal. It made her feel accepted. Genuinely interested in what he had to say, she was ready to linger on his words. He couldn't have been more unprepared for this moment. For years he'd been attracted to her. Long before she began dating Steve he'd hoped for a chance to do more than bake cakes near her. He never said anything to her about having an interest in dating her, which is why her boyfriend had the chance to build a life with her. "I've never told anyone about my insomnia. At night I lie awake in bed, listening to street noises, waiting for sleep."

"Well, I have panic attacks." It was easy to say now that it wasn't a secret. He pulled the chair near the desk closer to her and asked, "What does it feel like?" Dr. Morgan was the only other person who wanted to know about her attacks. "I feel like I'm unraveling. I can't breathe. I go numb."

"I bet that's scary, huh?"

"Yes. I'm always afraid that I'll die."

"You never seemed stressed out even when you're dealing with difficult customers."

"We've had plenty of those. The bakery brings me joy."

"I know what you mean. Sometimes I'm cranky from lack of sleep and I get here, start baking, and I feel better."

"Me too. Gathering all the ingredients for large batches of cake batter and following a recipe keeps me calm."

Kevin was easy to talk to. He'd been the best team leader she had ever worked with and from day one she trusted him. He invested a large sum of money into the bakery when Joan passed away. He wanted to help out with the finances and minor repairs of the bakery when Iris took over as owner. She thought he was genuinely kindhearted for the gesture, but now she knew that there was more behind his action. They worked well together, especially in a crisis. One evening an oven broke down while several cakes, due to be picked up the next day, were baking. Kevin noticed that the oven light, which was normally red, had suddenly shut off. He lept into action. He knew that transporting the cakes would be disastrous even though the other oven was adjacent to it. The last time he'd checked on the cakes there was about fifteen minutes left on the timer. This was a critical stage in the baking process. He immediately began tinkering around in the back of the oven's mechanisms and even burned his fingers and forearm while doing this. She was impressed that he was level-headed and determined to get the oven going again at least for the night so that customers who had paid for those specialty cakes wouldn't be disappointed. Less than fifteen minutes later the red oven light was back on and everyone on the bakery floor cheered for him. A few customers who were in the store front, deciding on which slices of cake they wanted to purchase also cheered when the oven was fixed.

Iris was jolted out of this memory by the touch of his hand on hers. He gently rubbed her palm with his fingertips as he held it. Not once had Kevin taken his eyes off her while he was in her office. She saw desire in his dark eyes and every muscle in her body stiffened. She braced herself for a kiss. Then he told her about his ex-girlfriend. "A few years I was heavily involved with woman I thought I'd marry someday. I loved her Jamaican accent more than anything else about her. We argued all the time over minor things. She didn't like that I kept forgetting to cap the toothpaste or that I had dirty socks on the floor instead of in the hamper. We weren't happy at all, but we were together for two years. I spent most nights working long hours here. It was better than being at home with her. One day I came home and saw that she'd packed all her belongings and moved out. I was relieved that she'd left. We never spoke again." Iris was staring at him. He enjoyed having her attention. He knew that she'd been with her boyfriend for several years.

He met Steve once after he'd broken up with his girlfriend. He wasn't impressed. He always felt that his boss deserved a better man. Someone like him. Kevin kissed the back of her hand. She was drawn to his compassion, openness. *Give in to the moment*. It was now or never. While holding her hand Kevin told her how he felt. "I care about you and whatever you need I'm here for you. You are the most beautiful, intelligent, and hardworking woman I've ever known." He stroked her other arm. "It's a privilege to work for you. I don't know what brought you here tonight, but I can see that you're unhappy. I'm just glad I've finally had the chance to say what I should've told you years ago."

Her muscles relaxed from his touch. It was gentle and loving. Across the desk they leaned in closer to each other. He pressed his lips against hers. They were full and soft. He rose from his seat and pulled her close. His heart raced. Her chest against his body aroused him. She'd hoped that when he kissed her face, lips, and neck, she'd feel something for him. She wanted sparks to ricochet off the walls to mirror his desire for her. His kisses weren't like Tina's. She imagined Tina there instead of him and pulled away from Kevin. "I can't do this." He didn't want it to end. Kissing and touching her felt wonderful. Kevin believed she felt overwhelmed by his sudden admission of interest in her. He could wait until she was ready to be with him. "It's ok. I understand."

They talked until sunrise. She missed several calls from Steve. He realized she wasn't coming back to the apartment when she didn't answer her cell phone. He was angry from being ignored, not knowing where she was and if she was safe. He had a hunch that she might be at the bakery, but stubbornness kept him from going there to look for her. If he discovered that his girlfriend had made out and spent the entire evening with another man in her office, he would've broken Kevin's jaw, yelled, and choked her for causing him pain. Relieved that he didn't answer, she left him the following message:
Hi, it's me. I slept at the bakery and I'm fine. I'll be home soon.
Kevin and Iris embraced and he stayed behind to open the bakery. She left before any of the others arrived to work. She avoided telling him that she wasn't interested in becoming involved with him. He was the perfect guy for

someone else. She wanted Tina. Her heart said it was ok. She thought of visiting Dr. Morgan to tell her everything she had experienced, but her therapist was unavailable. Her absence from the office was odd. Morgan took vacations twice a year and she'd already taken two this year. When she learned that Morgan would be out of the office for an entire week, she assumed that it had to be for a good reason. She had no other choice except to schedule an appointment with her for the following week.

She couldn't deal with trying to figure out how to tell Steve that she'd fallen for a woman. She imagined returning to the apartment, finding him there, looking pitiful, and blurting out *I'm in love with a woman!* She booked a room at a nice hotel not far from the bakery and sent Tina a text, telling her to meet her there. An hour later Iris felt her heart flutter when she heard a knock at the door. Tina smiled as she entered the room, held her left hand up, wiggled her ring finger, and said, "I broke off the engagement."

"I'm so glad to hear you say that."

"I was happy to return the ring."

"How'd he take the news?"

"Not good at all. He was groveling. It shocked me. He even said he was willing to amend the prenuptial agreement just to please me. He wanted to make things work and be married forever. All I could think about was you."

"I have to move out of my apartment."

"You can stay with me." They were sitting next to each other on the bed. Tina grabbed Iris' face, kissed it and her lips longingly. Desire helixed inside them. Iris stood up and let her bathrobe fall to the floor. They made love.

ENCOUNTER

She went home the next morning and was relieved that Steve had already left for work. On a torn piece of paper he scribbled a note: *We need to talk.* She balled it up and left it lying on the nightstand. She went to the storage room on the upper floor of the apartment complex and pulled out three large suitcases. It was a hassle to get the luggage back down to their apartment floor. But when she did, she flung clothing, shoes, and important documents inside them. She packed those suitcases tightly and they were too heavy to carry them all down one flight of stairs to the elevator. She dragged each suitcase out the apartment and down the stairs, leaving them near the elevator. Tina was in the car waiting for her. She'd offered assistance, but Iris wanted to do it alone. Get in and out of the apartment quickly. It would be better this way. She hadn't told Steve about Tina. He would eventually find out and in her opinion he only cared about himself so she didn't owe him any explanation.

He entered the apartment before she could drag the last suitcase out. *Breathe. Don't panic.* He was sweaty. He'd called off work, hoped she would be there when he returned from his run. "What's going on?" Iris wanted to say *this is what leaving you looks like.* But nothing came out. Her words were stifled by sheer anxiety coursing through every vein in her body. The look in his eyes paralyzed her movements, voice. In a soft tone, he said, "Don't do this to us." *Pick up the suitcase and run.* She gripped the handle on top and tried lifting it. "Need some help?" Hearing Tina's voice put her emotions at ease. Steve whipped his head around to see who it was. He recognized the woman from the bakery. "I could use a hand. This one is extremely heavy."

"Hold on a minute. Could you just leave and give us a moment here?"

"Nope. I'm not going anywhere. She needs my help." Tina walked toward Iris who was frozen in place in the living room. She feared things might get ugly. A wink from Tina made her feel safe.

"Listen, I don't know you that well, but we're in the middle of something here and it has nothing to do with you so I'm asking you kindly to please leave." She ignored him, although she sensed that he was pissed. Tina grabbed the suitcase, lifted it with ease, and said, "I've got it babe. Let's go."

"Babe? What the hell is going on here?" Steve tried to yank the suitcase from her grip. Tina held on as he tugged at it from the side. She raised the suitcase and gave him a hard shove with it. He stumbled backward a little. He clenched his jaw, tightened his lips, and charged at her. "Back off," Iris said and pushed him as she stood between them. Tina was ready to fight. They were standing by the door.

"You're not leaving here until we straighten this out!" he said. Iris smacked his hand away as he reached for her arm.

"Nothing you say can change how I feel." Tina put a free hand on her shoulder, motioning Iris to leave. "We're done."

"Would you stop being crazy? You're just mixed up right now." The women were holding hands. Iris stopped in the doorway, turned to look at Steve, and said, "She makes me happy."

"Is this some kind of joke?" He took off his shoe and hurled it at the door as she was closing it.

Her side of the closet was mostly empty. A few clothes and pairs of shoes remained there. In the bathroom her fragrance, makeup, and toiletries, things he'd grown accustomed to seeing each morning he staggered into the bathroom not fully awake, her things that he didn't mind having around were gone. Steve felt like a bulldozer had run over him as he raced to the storage area on the upper level to find that she'd taken the full set of luggage he'd bought her for an anniversary gift. He dropped to his knees and burst into tears, putting his face in the palms of his hands. He couldn't accept she'd moved out. No chance to prove to her that he was a good man. He stood up and slammed the door to the storage unit. Inside the apartment he pressed her number on his cell phone to tell her off, but hung up before the call went through. After all he'd done leading up to the moment she left with another woman he realized there was no point in trying to get her back.

In the days that passed after Steve returned home to the apartment to find Iris moving out, he became extremely angry with her. He couldn't accept the fact that now she was a lesbian. One night he called her number repeatedly until she finally answered. As soon as she said Hello he screamed at her for leaving in the manner in which she did. "I can't believe that after almost five years of creating a life together and with all the history we've shared, which goes all the way back to before you were the owner of the bakery when I worked as Joan's accountant, you claimed you loved me, now you're throwing this all away?" She let out a heavy sigh. "It's over. You need to let go. And stop harassing me."

175

"I can't. I was probably wrong for spending so much time with buddies from work and piling on more clients every year, but this was just a phase that we could've worked through. I wasn't a monster. I was willing to do whatever it took to fix things. At one point you were too."

"There was a time when I would've done anything for you. You never gave any consideration to my needs. I was suffering from deep depression and panic attacks, but I continued to manage the bakery and responsibilities at the apartment, acting like there was nothing wrong with me. When I needed you most, you abandoned me like road kill. You were the reason why I woke in the middle of the night, dazed and soaking wet from perspiring heavily in my sleep. Why you checked out on me? On us? Doesn't matter now." He shook his head a little as if by doing this he could somehow avoid reality. She was done with him.

"You're not really a lesbian. Are you?"

"I'm happy with her."

"Remember our date at the museum and how well we got along the entire day? That day was magical and I can't believe that you're acting completely clueless to everything I'm saying to you right now."

Steve pleaded his case to her for over an hour. During his soliloquy she drifted off to sleep. He hung up when she didn't respond to his questions or him repeatedly calling her name. The next morning she laughed hysterically over the incident. She noticed her cell phone on the floor next to the bed where she'd dropped it after falling asleep. She thought it was ridiculous of him to keep ranting on and on long after she shared that

176

arrangements were made for movers to collect belongings she'd left behind in the apartment. Her relationship with Tina was kept secret for a year. Other workers in the bakery suspected they were a couple. Sometimes they were affectionate in front of others. No one had the nerve to ask them about it. One day Kevin walked in on them kissing when he needed her signature on a receipt for a shipment of supplies. He never mentioned the moment they shared in her office.

FORGIVENESS

They hadn't spoken to each other in months. The last time they did, it wasn't a pleasant conversation between best friends. Both blamed each other for creating the reason behind their anger and frustration. Lacy finally worked up the nerve to call Rene and leave a message for her to meet at Mr. Hoagie for lunch. It was a food truck parked near the lake and one of their favorite places to grab a sandwich and then gossip. The next day she waited in her car for Rene to show up. She didn't know if Rene would come because she never returned her call. She missed her best friend immensely and she felt life without her was flat. It didn't matter that prior to their fall out they didn't spend a lot of time together. When they did, it was always great fun. They picked up right where they left off like close friends often do. She told Rene to meet her at the truck at two o'clock. She looked at her watch and noticed it was a quarter past two. Disappointed she believed there was no hope of ever having her best friend back in her life. Time apart gave Lacy a chance to reflect on their friendship. She never intended to make Rene feel like she was one of her patients. She also never wanted her to be hurt by some guy who was only using her for attention while he tried to mend a broken relationship with his girlfriend.

Someone was honking a car horn and the sound came from behind her. She frowned and then softened her face when she realized that it was Rene. Late. She looked amazing as she got out of her car. She was slimmer, although she didn't need to lose any weight. She'd been working out hard in the gym. Her arms were muscular, toned, and she had a smaller waist.

Lacy got out the car and smiled at her best friend. Rene was doing the same thing as she walked toward her. They embraced for an extended time and even swayed a little back and forth like kids do when they're happy. "It's been such a long time."

"I know. I've missed you." Lacy felt almost ready to cry over a warm greeting. Rene smiled in her arms. "I'm so sorry for everything Lace." She hadn't called her Lace since they were in college. She knew that she'd forgiven her and that this reunion would help restore things between them back to normal. "I never meant for you to be hurt by what happened," Lacy said. "I know. This is the perfect spot for us to talk. I'm starving too." They walked to the food truck and ordered a foot long hoagie to share. The weather was perfect for eating outdoors. Lacy began talking to Rene about all the changes in her life. "When you and I argued, it broke my heart. I knew that what you needed was for me to remove my doctor hat and consider you as the greatest friend I've ever had. It's what you deserve from me. Now I understand how you felt and it wasn't until I took time away from being a therapist that I begin to really feel whole again. I didn't treat any patients for over three months. The practice was interfering with my ability to connect with special people like you and moments I was missing in life. I felt terrible about not being the friend that would simply come out and say yes, *Rene that jerk accountant that dumped you is nothing but an arrogant loser and he doesn't deserve your attention at all.* But I was too rigid to let go of a professional opinion that means nothing without your friendship." Rene put a hand on top of Lacy's as she continued to listen to her speak. "My heart told me that you would never do anything to jeopardize my career. I shouldn't have let my practice interrupt the true friendship we share. Please forgive me."

"Of course I do. And I hope that you can forgive me too. I should've reached out to you sooner, but I didn't know what to say after hitting you and things escalated the way they did. You've always been the greatest friend to me. I blamed you because I wasn't willing to accept the truth about myself that once again I had chosen another unavailable man. As soon as I learned this, I should've walked away from him. I didn't and that's my fault. Putting you in a predicament where you felt the need to choose between your ethical boundaries and your loyalty to me as a friend was highly selfish of me. I was wrong. I've given myself a chance to heal, to deal with my personal issues alone. I've relied on you to pull me out of the gutter far too long."

"No matter what, I'm always going to be here for you."

"I know."

"So have you become a gymrat?" They laughed at Lacy's question. Rene confirmed that she exercised to relieve stress and distract herself from Steve. "You know that he tried to rekindle the relationship."

"I'm not surprised. What happened?" Rene didn't feel like Lacy had her therapist cap on. It felt normal. Sitting on a bench in the park, eating good food, and gossiping about things that had transpired in their lives was the only thing that mattered to them. They renewed a sense of trust and loyalty in a friendship that spanned twenty years. The women knew that they would never let anything interfere with it. "One night he called me, whining about how his girlfriend had moved out the apartment after they had an argument. Apparently he told her that he knew about her therapy sessions with you, but he didn't tell her how he found out."

"He probably lied to her about it."

"Oh, there's more." Rene had a smirk on her face.

"Go on."

"While they were arguing, he says she pulled out her phone and began texting someone. Seconds later the door opened and a woman walked in. It was her girlfriend."

"Are you kidding me?"

"Nope. And he was devastated by the fact that she left him for a woman." Lacy giggled and said, "I didn't know she liked women." "He went on and on about his hurt feelings, how wrong she was for leaving him. Listening to him whine made my stomach turn. From that moment on I wanted nothing to do with him."

"Good for you.

"I told him that his circumstances were unfortunate and then I made up an excuse to end the call."

"I bet he was sour. Was that the last time you spoke to him?"

"No way. He was persistent. And lonely. He was surprised when I told him that I didn't want to go out to dinner with him."

"I'm sure it crushed his ego."

"His pity party was pathetic. I wasn't concerned about his hurt feelings over a breakup. I couldn't allow myself to be there for him, not for him or any man that didn't truly respect and value me."

Lacy listened and occasionally nodded as Rene spoke. She was proud of her. Rene grabbed empty drinking cups and the sandwich wrapping and dumped them in a nearby trash can. The beach area near the lake was filled with people lying out, running or walking in the sand, enjoying the sunshine. "Someday we'll both find the right man." They sat in silence on that bench for two hours. Before leaving the park they set a new date to meet for lunch and workouts together.

THE AUTHOR

Valerie O'Brien is a writer, author of short stories and poet. She is a Chicago native who has been writing poetry for many years. Her work has been featured in *Spirits* and *The Haiku Journal*. *Numb* is her first book. Visit her at www.v-obrien.com.

www.ingramcontent.com/pod-product-compliance
Lightning Source LLC
Chambersburg PA
CBHW030255130626
46549CB00002B/534